Also by Catherine Hapka

Dolphin
SUMMER

Also by Catherine Hapka

Heart of a Dolphin

Dolphin Dreams

Dolphin Summer

CATHERINE HAPKA

Scholastic Inc.

The publisher does not have any control over and does not assume any responsibility for author or third-party websites or their content.

No part of this publication may be reproduced, stored in a retrieval system, or transmitted in any form or by any means, electronic, mechanical, photocopying, recording, or otherwise, without written permission of the publisher. For information regarding permission, write to Scholastic Inc., Attention: Permissions Department, 557 Broadway, New York, NY 10012.

ISBN 978-1-338-13644-9

10 9 8 7 6 5 4 3 2 1   18 19 20 21 22

Printed in the U.S.A.   40

First printing 2018

Book design by Mary Claire Cruz

For anyone who has ever worked to
save something beautiful

And for Ellen, who's always up for
an adventure

Dolphins had seemed almost magical to me for as long as I could remember. With their sleek bodies and playful personalities and the graceful way they leaped out of the water, they were just plain amazing. All I'd ever wanted was to be near them. Because then maybe some of that magic would rub off on me. But even though, technically, I lived on an island, it wasn't exactly easy to find dolphins in New York City.

"Too bad there aren't any dolphins at the aquarium anymore," I murmured with a sigh. I leaned on the railing and watched a walrus swim lazily back and forth. He was huge, and looked ridiculous whenever he waddled onto the artificial rocks in his enclosure. But in the water he was sleek and graceful. Not as graceful as the sharks across the way, though, or the otters next door, and definitely not as graceful as a dolphin.

The lack of dolphins didn't stop me from coming to the aquarium as often as I could. There were plenty of other interesting creatures to see: sea lions and penguins and eels and sharks and rays. Dolphins might have been my favorite, but I loved all the creatures of the sea. I wanted to be a marine biologist when I grew up, even though everyone said that was a crazy goal for an ordinary girl from Brooklyn.

The walrus stuck his head out of the water, staring around with droplets clinging to his bristly whiskers. I was smiling at his funny expression when I felt my phone vibrate in the pocket of my shorts.

It was a text from my friend Julia.

Hey Lily! Wassup? We saw a frog in the lake today and thought of you. Well I did, but Amber got freaked out, haha...

"His name's Archie," a boy's voice said beside me.

I jumped, startled. I'd been so busy glaring at the text that I hadn't even noticed anyone coming up beside me.

"Who are you?" I blurted out, taking a step back.

"Sorry." He waved a hand toward the display. "I didn't mean to scare you. I, uh, thought you might be looking up more info about the walrus." The boy's earnest brown eyes darted to my phone, then back to my face. "I was just telling you, his name is Archie—short for Archibald."

"Oh." I blinked at the boy. He was around my age—twelve—with close-cropped dark hair. He wore khaki shorts and a short-sleeved button-down shirt, which seemed a little odd—most of the boys in my neighborhood lived in jeans or athletic shorts and T-shirts all summer.

Before I could say anything else, a woman bustled over to us. She was dressed in khaki shorts, too, with a tidy white pin on her shirt pocket that read *Susan: Water-Quality Technician*. I'd seen her once or twice during previous visits to the aquarium, though I'd never been up close enough to read her name tag. Or to see her expression, either, which at this moment was crabby and impatient.

"You," she snapped, pointing at the boy. "They're looking for you in the lab. What are you doing out here?" She turned her suspicious glare toward me, as if blaming me for distracting him.

"Sorry," the boy muttered. After shooting me one last look, he scurried off and disappeared around the corner behind the gift shop.

The woman ignored me as she turned away and walked back over to the otter exhibit. I watched out of the corner of my eye, fascinated to see her at work. She grabbed a couple of plastic bottles out of a bucket and then reached into the tank, scooping up some of the water.

"Hey there, Miz Giordano." A deep, raspy voice startled me out of my observations.

This time I recognized the voice. It belonged to Eddy, who had worked at the gift shop for as long as I'd been coming to the aquarium. I turned to see his crooked-toothed grin greeting me.

I smiled back. Eddy reminded me of my grandpa Rocco, who'd died last year. Most people probably wouldn't think they were alike at all—Eddy was tall and black and talkative, and Grandpa Rocco had been short and white and quiet. But there was something about the happy crinkles around Eddy's eyes and the way he laughed that always made me glad to see him, just like my grandpa.

He leaned on the fence beside me, watching Archie swim back and forth across his tank. "Don't think I didn't see you flirting with that boy, Lily," Eddy said with a chuckle, waggling one knobby-knuckled finger at me.

"What?" I stood up straight, shoving his finger away. "Eddy!"

He laughed again. "I don't blame you. He's a handsome fella."

I could feel myself blushing, though I was laughing, too. "Don't be crazy," I said. "I'm only twelve! Anyway, I don't even know who he is. He just started talking to me." I hesitated, not wanting to bring on more teasing, but curious. "Um, does he work here or something?"

"Yes, just started when school let out for the summer a couple weeks ago." Eddy scratched his chin. "He's a student what-d'you-call-it—intern—back there in the research lab. His daddy is one of the scientists, and—"

"Eddy!" Susan the water-quality tech had finished collecting her samples. Now she was walking toward us, bucket of bottles in hand and eyes narrowed. "Shouldn't you be at work? You were taking a break the last time I came out front, too."

"Sorry, ma'am." Eddy took a step back. "Just

sneaked out to say hello to Miz Lily here." He winked at me. "See you later."

"Bye." I waved as he headed back to the gift shop, which was just across the path. When I turned, Susan was staring at me suspiciously.

"Are you here alone?" she demanded. "How old are you?"

"I—um . . ." Even though I wasn't doing anything wrong, I was suddenly nervous, and unsure where to put my hands.

Just then I heard someone calling my name. Glancing over with relief, I saw Nia Watts striding toward us from the direction of the food carts, two ice pops in her hands. Nia was a little over six feet tall and thin as an eel, with a big, wild Afro that always had its tips frosted in funky colors. Right now it was mostly electric blue, with a few spots of red and yellow near her ears.

"Lily! There you are." Nia gave me an ice-pop-purple-stained grin as she handed me one of the frozen treats. "You're lucky I found you before I ate both of these."

"Thanks." I shot a slightly nervous glance toward Susan, but she was already backing off, pretending to be busy rearranging the bottles in her bucket as she sidled away. My mouth twisted into a tiny smile. Nia's loud, artistic style could be a little intimidating if you didn't know her.

That was what people told me, anyway. Nia had gone to school with my oldest brother, Ricky, and since he was almost twelve whole years older than me, I'd known her pretty much since I was born. For the past few years my parents had paid her to watch me in the summer while they were both at work. By this summer I thought I was probably old enough to stay by myself—I mean, Julia had started babysitting her younger sister after school this past spring—but I didn't really mind hanging out with Nia. I was pretty sure she liked having me around, too. We spent most of our time at her rented art studio, where she created strange, beautiful sculptures out of metal and glass and sometimes clay or feathers or whatever else she felt like using. But I could usually convince her to take a break from work for what we called field trips—and of course, my favorite field trip was to the aquarium.

"Who were you talking to?" Nia asked, twisting her hand to lick a melty spot on her ice pop before it dripped down onto her tie-dyed sundress.

"Hmm?" I glanced around, but the water tech had disappeared. "Oh. Nobody."

Nia shrugged. "Okay. Ready to split? I need to get back to work, and you have some reading to do."

"Right." My heart sank slightly. "Um, okay. Thanks for bringing me."

She smiled and rumpled my dark hair. "No worries. You know I like it here. Very inspiring." She winked. "I might do something with penguins next; what do you think?"

"Sounds good." I fell into step beside her as we headed for the exit, though I had to take two scurrying steps for every one of her long-legged ones.

Outside, we headed for the West Eighth Street subway stop. Almost everyone else was heading the other way, toward the Coney Island beach and boardwalk. There were teenagers, excited little kids with parents or nannies in tow, and several pairs of bright-eyed old ladies dressed in one-piece swimsuits with rubber caps over their hair.

The F train wasn't very crowded. Nia and I found seats at one end of the car. She pulled off her backpack and dug into it, eventually coming up with a battered copy of *The Call of the Wild*.

"Here you go," she said, handing it to me.

Soon she was leaning back with her eyes closed and earbuds in, humming along to whatever was playing on her phone. I opened the book to the page I'd turned down and sighed.

There wasn't really anything wrong with the book. Actually, I was mostly enjoying it. I just wished I'd decided to read it on my own instead of being forced to by my parents. My school always supplied a summer reading list, which was supposed to be voluntary. But this year it was mandatory for me, thanks to the B-minus I'd received in sixth-grade English.

Which is so not fair, I thought, staring at the words on the page without really seeing them. *I only messed up on that one test because I was working so hard on my research project for science. Besides, if Ozzy came home with a B-minus in English, they'd throw him a party.*

My almost-seventeen-year-old brother wasn't much of a student, but then again he didn't have to be. Everyone already knew that he'd be going to work for my dad's plumbing business as soon as he graduated from high school, just like Ricky had. Dad had already changed the logo on his truck to Giordano and Sons, even though only one of his two sons was technically a full-time partner so far.

But me? I was different. In fifth grade, I'd won a big end-of-the-year award for my essay about *Island of the Blue Dolphins*. Ever since then, my family was convinced that I would be an English teacher someday. No matter how many times I told them I liked science better . . .

I managed to read part of a chapter by the time we got off at our usual stop, the Smith–Ninth Street station. But as we started climbing down the zillion steps that led from the elevated platform to the street, my mind wandered back to that kid I'd met at the aquarium. How cool would it be to be a summer intern there?

"Lily! Hey!"

I jerked out of my thoughts. Clattering up the steps toward us was a trio of girls from my class—Olivia Choi and a couple of her friends. Olivia was one of the most popular girls at school, but she was nice to everyone. I didn't know her that well, though, since she lived way over in the nicest part of Park Slope and I was across the canal in Carroll Gardens.

"Hi," I said shyly.

"Hey, you're Vanessa's sister, right?" Nia pointed

at one of the other girls. "I did silk-screening at your birthday party last year, remember?"

That was typical. Nia seemed to know everyone in Brooklyn. At least, she managed to run into someone she knew practically everywhere we went.

The girl nodded eagerly, returning Nia's friendly smile. "Yeah, that was cool," she said. "I still have the T-shirt I made—I love it!"

"Dope." Nia grinned. "So where are you ladies headed?"

"Street fair in Brooklyn Heights." Olivia glanced at me. "Want to come, Lily?"

"I can't," I said quickly, before Nia could say anything. "Um, I told Nia I'd help her with something this afternoon."

"Okay, maybe some other time." Olivia smiled at me and Nia, and then one of the others squealed at the sound of the train clattering in on the tracks overhead, and then they were flying off up the stairs laughing and calling to one another.

Nia was watching me, one eyebrow quirked up in that way only she seemed able to do. "Don't you want to go to the street fair?" she asked, then grinned. "You know I'd cover for you with your folks about the reading."

"No, it's okay." I started walking down the steps again. "I mean, I didn't feel like walking around in the heat anymore."

She didn't answer, which is one of the good things about Nia. My parents would have kept bugging me, telling me that just because Julia and Amber were away it didn't mean I couldn't have fun with other friends.

But Nia didn't say anything until we were out of the station and on the bridge crossing the Gowanus Canal. "Hey, mind if we stop off for some supplies?" she asked, nodding toward the big-box hardware store up ahead.

"Do I have to come in?" I asked.

She smiled. "You can sit by the water if you

want, mermaid girl," she said. "Got your phone on you?"

I pulled it out. "Got it."

"Good. Call me if you get kidnapped or anything. Better yet, text me—that way I can decide if it's important enough to come rescue you."

I was still smiling at that as she hurried off across the huge parking lot toward the store entrance. Nia loved to joke about the stuff other people worried about. Her jokes had always made my dad frown and Ricky roll his eyes, but I thought she was funny.

At the far end of the parking lot was a little grassy area with a fence bordering its outside edge. On the other side of that was the canal.

I leaned on the fence, staring down at the murky water. Even I had to admit that the Gowanus Canal wasn't the most beautiful thing in the world. Right now I could see various bits of unidentifiable trash floating past, and right beneath where I was standing, a white plastic bag was caught in the rocks at the canal's edge.

But there was still something kind of magical about it, about the constantly moving water and the breeze and the gulls that were usually wheeling overhead. Because I knew that the canal led out to the bay and then beyond that to the ocean, where so many fabulous creatures lived.

I stood and wandered along the fence line, watching little ripples caused by the slow-moving current. I couldn't see anything moving under the surface, but imagined schools of fish darting around, maybe even a jellyfish or a crab . . .

Eventually I hit the spot where the fence made a left-hand turn. There was a good-sized inlet jutting into the land there, the kind of place where you could park a large boat or something, though I'd never seen a boat there.

I glanced down and was just about to turn around and wander back the other way when something made me stop short. Was my imagination swimming away with me? Because I could have sworn there was something moving just under the water . . .

"What the heck . . . ?" I muttered, leaning halfway over the fence for a better look. Sunlight sparkled off the oily surface, making me squint.

But yes—there! Something was definitely moving underwater.

Visions of mermaids danced through my head, making me smile. It almost seemed more likely I'd spot a mythical creature in this toxic sludge than a real one. But then a shape emerged from the water, and I gasped.

Because there in front of me, right here in familiar old Brooklyn, in the polluted waters of the Gowanus Canal . . . was a real, honest-to-goodness dolphin!

2

For a second all I could do was stare. By the time my brain kicked in again, the dolphin had dived back down below the surface.

"Oh my gosh," I gasped out at last. "Oh my gosh!"

I leaned over the fence and clapped my hands, hoping to attract the creature's attention. Had I really seen a dolphin just now? Or were the fumes from the canal going to my head?

No—there it was again! This time the dolphin only peeked out briefly before ducking back underwater. But I'd seen it—I'd really seen it!

My heart pounded, and I let out a soft whistle. A year or so ago I'd looked up dolphin sounds on the Internet and practiced a few for a while, though I'd never told anybody—I'd known that Julia and Amber would have never let me hear the end of it if they had known, let alone my brothers. They would all think it was goofy and weird, like a little kid barking at the family dog or something. But now the squeaks and chirps and whistles came back to me, and I ran through all the sounds I could remember.

Finally the dolphin surfaced again, this time staring at me with her big, sad, dark eyes. I stared back, holding my breath. She was so beautiful!

Then she thrashed and spun around in the water. She started to swim toward the main part of the canal. But before she reached the mouth of the inlet, she stopped, let out a chirp, and then turned back, disappearing again beneath the greasy surface.

My hands were trembling as I pulled out my phone. I couldn't imagine trying to text in that condition, so I just hit the little phone next to her name to call Nia.

"Hey, thought I told you to text," she said when she answered. "Must be an extra-scary kidnapper."

"No," I blurted out, my eyes still scanning the iridescent water of the inlet. "It's a dolphin!"

"Huh? I don't get it," Nia said. "Listen, can this wait? Because I'm almost done here, and—"

"No, Nia, listen," I said. "I just saw a dolphin! Out here in the canal!"

She was silent for a second. "Lily . . ."

I could tell she didn't believe me. "Hold on," I said.

I switched over to the camera, then waited. It took just long enough that I started again to doubt what I'd seen myself.

There she was! The dolphin surfaced, probably just to breathe, since she went back under almost immediately. But I'd managed to get a pretty good photo, which I immediately texted to Nia.

Then I switched back to phone mode. "Whoa,"

she said when I came on the line. "Hang on, I'll be right out."

Soon both of us were hanging on the fence, watching and waiting for the dolphin's next appearance. "What do we do?" I asked her.

Nia always knew what to do. This turned out to be no exception. "We need to contact the authorities," she said. "It shouldn't be here. The canal isn't healthy for any living thing."

"No kidding." I glanced at the nearest clump of floating trash. "She must have swum in and got lost. Or maybe she's sick—or hurt!" I clutched the railing harder as horrible possibilities raced through my head. "What if she's dying?"

Just then the dolphin surfaced again, this time floating there looking at us for a moment before diving down. "Looks like she's still kicking right now." Nia was scrolling through her phone. "Don't panic, okay? Let me just make a call . . ."

It turned out to take more than one call. Nia ended up explaining the situation to at least three different people before she wandered far enough away that I couldn't hear her clearly anymore. I stayed by the inlet fence watching for the dolphin.

Then I heard voices behind me. I ignored them at first, figuring it was just customers from the hardware store heading back to their cars or something. But then they got even closer, and I turned around and saw three boys from my neighborhood coming my way.

In the lead was my friend Amber's cousin Zach, who was two years older than us and lived in the other half of their brownstone. I recognized his friends from seeing them around the neighborhood, though I wasn't sure of their names.

"Hey, check it out—it's Lily Left-Behind," Zach said with a smirk.

"Huh?" said one of his friends, a skinny kid with white-blond hair and a sunburned nose. He was kicking a stone back and forth between his feet like a soccer ball.

"Lily's friends with my cousin Amber," Zach told the other boys. "But she and their other friend went off to summer camp without her." He pretended to wipe tears from his eyes. "Boo-hoo, hope you're not too upset, Lily Left-Behind."

I rolled my eyes, trying not to let his obnoxiousness bother me. What did he really know about that whole situation? Probably nothing.

"Whatever, Zach," I said, trying to sound bored and cool and unimpressed, like Olivia Choi or Nia might. "If you don't have anything useful to say—"

"Hey, check it out!" Zach's other friend was at the inlet fence pointing into the water. "I just saw, like, a shark or something out there!"

"Yeah, right," the blond kid said with a snort.

"It's a dolphin," I corrected him before I could stop myself.

Zach looked surprised. "For real? In the canal?"

Soon all three boys were leaning so far over the fence that I was half fearing and half hoping they'd fall in. When the dolphin surfaced for breath, they let out a whoop.

"It's for real!" the blond kid shouted. "How'd that thing get in here?"

The third boy pulled out his phone and snapped a photo, even though the dolphin was back underwater by then. "This is wild! Hey, get it to come up here again so I can get a good shot."

Zach scooped up a handful of gravel from the drainage ditch leading under the fence. "Here, dolphin dolphin dolphin!" he called, tossing the gravel at the last spot where the dolphin had surfaced.

"Stop that!" I cried.

He barely spared me a disdainful glance before scooping up more gravel. "Make me, Lily Left-Behind." Then he tossed that gravel into the water, too.

My heart thumped in my chest. How was I going to stop them? They were bigger than me, and meaner, and there were three of them . . .

"Hey, what are you hooligans doing over here?" Suddenly Nia was back, larger than life as usual, glaring at the boys. "Did you throw something at that poor dolphin?"

Zach and his friends stared at her, seeming mesmerized by her tallness, her anger, her general awesomeness. "Uh . . ." the blond kid said.

"We were just trying to get its attention," Zach whined.

Nia frowned, crossing her arms over her chest. "Well, maybe it doesn't think you're worth paying attention to," she said. "Ever think of that, baby boy?"

Zach glared at her, clearly not liking the nickname. "Whatever. It's no big deal."

"Not yet, maybe," Nia replied warningly. "Just test me, honey . . ."

They grumbled and swore a little, but they were already backing away, looking nervous. I hid my relieved smile until they'd turned and hightailed it across the parking lot toward Ninth Street, banging on the hoods of parked cars as they went.

Nia seemed to forget about the boys instantly, all smiles again as she turned to face me. "I finally found the right people to talk to," she reported. "Someone from the aquarium is coming out right now to see the dolphin."

After that we waited, watching the dolphin and speculating about how she'd gotten there and what would happen next. Nia pulled a sketchpad and a charcoal pencil out of her backpack and started outlining a dolphin leaping from the water.

"That's good," I said, peering at the drawing over her shoulder. "But the dorsal fin is too far forward—see? It should be here."

"Thanks." She rubbed out the fin and redrew it. "Better?"

"Perfect." As she continued to sketch, I stepped closer to the fence again. The dolphin poked her head out right away, as if she'd been waiting for me. Shooting a quick look back at Nia, who seemed focused on her sketch, I sucked in a breath and then let out a soft whistle.

The dolphin reacted, lifting her head higher. Then she dived back underwater.

I waited. When she resurfaced, I was ready with a series of clicks with another whistle at the end.

"Hey." I didn't realize Nia had come closer until I heard her voice right at my ear. "That's pretty good. When did you learn to speak Dolphin?"

I turned to face her, blushing. "I didn't think you were listening."

"I was." She gestured toward the dolphin, whose nose and eyes were just poking up from the dark water. "So was he, looks like."

"Yeah. Except I think she's a she, not a he," I said. "Female dolphins are smaller and slimmer than males, and this one looks fairly small."

Nia nodded. "Sorry, girl," she called to the dolphin. "Hey, Lily, how do you say sorry in Dolphinese?"

I laughed. "I'm not sure. But let me try . . ."

With Nia egging me on, I ran through my entire repertoire of dolphin sounds. I even made up a few new ones. The dolphin appeared to enjoy it or at least be intrigued. She stayed at the surface for longer and longer, seeming to listen and even letting out an occasional chirp or whistle herself.

I was teaching Nia how to make a few of the sounds when a car pulled up to the edge of the parking lot closest to us. Three people climbed out—a man and two women. "Is the dolphin still here?" one of the women asked, hurrying toward us.

"Right down there." Nia pointed. "I'm Nia Watts, and this is Lily Giordano. She's the one who spotted the dolphin."

"Nice to meet you both." The man had a nice smile, and didn't seem fazed at all to be talking to a kid and a wild-haired artist. "I'm Dr. Hernandez, one of the research biologists from the aquarium.

This is my colleague Dr. Gallagher." He gestured at one of the women, then the other. "And that's Ms. Khan."

"I'm just a lab tech," Ms. Khan said cheerfully. "I'm mostly here because my car was handy and had a full tank of gas."

Dr. Hernandez chuckled. "Don't sell yourself short," he told her with a wink. "You've got the best camera on your phone, too."

The others chuckled along with him, including Nia. But I was too nervous to laugh.

"What's going to happen to her?" I asked. "She shouldn't be in the canal, should she?"

"No, she shouldn't." Dr. Gallagher shook her head. "But let's not get ahead of ourselves—we need to see what we're working with here."

I wasn't sure what that meant. But I stood back as the aquarium crew lined up at the fence. It wasn't long before the dolphin surfaced again.

Ms. Khan gasped. "Oh, she's lovely!"

"Yes." Dr. Hernandez pulled out his phone and tapped something into it. "Looks healthier than I was expecting."

Nia and I traded a look. I guess she read the worry on my face, because she cleared her throat. "What were you expecting?"

"You never know." Dr. Gallagher was watching Ms. Khan, who was snapping photos with her phone. "Make sure you get some of it surfacing," she told the other woman. "Maybe some video?"

Ms. Khan nodded. "On it."

"Come on." Nia tugged gently on my arm. "Let's give them some space."

We backed away, perching on one of the picnic tables set up in the shady part of the grass. The three aquarium people spent a few more minutes observing the dolphin, taking more pictures, and talking to one another in low voices.

Finally Dr. Hernandez came toward us. "Thanks for calling us, young ladies," he said with a kind smile. "The dolphin looks relatively healthy at this point. We're going to give her a chance to find her way back out to sea on her own."

"What?" I blurted out. "You mean you're just going to leave her here, in the stinky canal?"

The scientist stuck his hands in his pockets. "For a little while, yes," he said, meeting my eye in a serious way that few adults bothered to do. As if he was talking to me as an equal, instead of a kid. I may not have liked what he was saying, but I found myself liking him.

"But what if she can't find her way out?" I asked. "She can't just stay here, can she?"

"No, she can't stay indefinitely." Dr. Hernandez glanced toward the water, then back at me. "But we can give her a day or two to figure things out. If that doesn't happen, then we'll intervene."

I wasn't sure what that meant, exactly. But something about Dr. Hernandez made me think I could trust him. So I just nodded and watched as the aquarium people climbed back in their car and drove away.

3

At dinner that night I picked at my food, distracted by thoughts of the dolphin. Nia and I had stayed for a couple of hours after the aquarium people left. Nia had said that was okay as long as I read my book and she worked on sketching ideas for her next sculpture. I'd sat on the grass right by the fence, not wanting to miss any movements by the dolphin.

But finally we'd had to leave. Nia had Dr. Hernandez's e-mail and phone number from when she'd called, and she'd promised to let me know right away if she heard anything from the aquarium.

Thinking of that, I carefully slid my phone out of my pocket, keeping it below the edge of the table so my family wouldn't see. We weren't supposed to have phones on at dinner, though Ozzy broke that rule all the time so he could text with his girlfriend.

There were no new messages from Nia, but there was one from Amber:

Check it out—tuna casserole for dinner at the mess hall tonight! Jules almost barfed, lol!

I grimaced and clicked off the phone without bothering to look at the photo Amber had included. My mom glanced over just in time to see my expression.

"You okay, Lily?" she asked with concern. "Something wrong with the manicotti?"

"No—it's good." I quickly took a big bite, hoping to avoid further questions by chewing.

No such luck. Dad and Ozzy had turned to look at me now, too. "Yeah, you look depressed," Ozzy observed in his usual know-it-all way. "Still bummed out about your friends going off to camp without you, huh?"

"No," I said quickly, not wanting that whole topic to start up again. "Actually, I was just thinking about this dolphin I saw in the canal today."

My father's bushy eyebrows shot up. "The canal?" he said, leaning forward with his elbows on the tablecloth and his fork halfway to his mouth. "Thought I told you to stay away from that cesspool."

"A dolphin?" my mother said at the same time. "Really?"

"Yeah, right, sure you saw a dolphin." Ricky had been shoveling food steadily into his mouth, but now he finally looked up just long enough to roll his eyes at me. My oldest brother was practically a carbon copy of our father—square jaw, thick, wavy dark hair, broad shoulders. With a few more pounds on Ricky and a little less gray around my dad's temples, they could be mistaken for identical twins.

"No, I'm serious." I hadn't meant to tell them about the dolphin at all—it wasn't the type of thing that would interest them—but now I was determined to make them believe me. "Nia saw it, too—she's the one who called the aquarium." I quickly ran through the gist of the story, leaving out the part where Nia let me wait alone outside the store.

That didn't stop my dad's expression from growing darker. "That Nia should know better than to let you near the canal," he growled.

With effort, I managed not to grimace. "That Nia" might as well be her name as far as my father was concerned.

"Your father is right," my mother said, standing up to dish out more salad to Ricky and Dad. "It's better to stay away from that filthy canal."

"It's better for dolphins to stay away from it, too," I pointed out. "That's why Nia and I wanted to help."

"It's all your fault, Ma, you know," Ozzy said with a grin. "It's that salt water in your veins that polluted Lily's mind when she was born. That's why she's so crazy about dolphins and stuff."

"Yeah. Good thing we were immune." Ricky raised his arm from his dinner just long enough to bump fists with Ozzy.

It was a familiar family joke, and even my father chuckled. While he'd been born and raised within six blocks of this very house, my mother wasn't from here. She'd grown up in a beach town in New Jersey, but she'd gone to college in Manhattan and met Dad at a house party right here in Brooklyn. Within months they were married—a true romance, according to all my aunts and uncles.

So maybe my family was right. Maybe I'd inherited my love of the sea from my mother.

And maybe it had been a mistake to mention the dolphin, I thought as my brothers started joking around about Mom's past and she smiled and shook her head. They already seemed to have forgotten about what I'd just told them, or maybe they just didn't think it was important. Either way, I should have known they wouldn't understand.

A couple of hours later, I was alone in my tiny room at the back of the apartment. It was hardly bigger than a broom closet, but I loved it because it was all mine and nobody was allowed to come in without knocking. Every inch of wall space was plastered with interesting things—what Mom jokingly called "Lily's wallpaper." There was a chart of Atlantic Ocean fish, a decorated crab shell that I'd bought on the Coney Island boardwalk, pictures torn from magazines or printed off the Internet of dolphins, whales, jellyfish, and more. And of course there was my favorite poster, which hung in the place of honor right over my bed. It featured a pod of dolphins leaping out of the water at sunset, and I touched it every night before I went to sleep.

Now I stared at it, wondering what the dolphin in the canal was doing right now. Or maybe she wasn't in the canal anymore. Maybe the scientists were right and she'd found her way back out to her pod.

Dolphins are supposed to be one of the smartest animals out there, I reminded myself, wandering over to the room's single window. *I bet she figured out how to get home.*

I stared out, wishing I could see the canal from here. But all I could see was the building across the alley and the sloped roof of the first-floor apartment below. If only I had the guts to climb out the window onto that rooftop. Then all I would have to do was slide down the pipe on the corner of the building and walk a few blocks, and I'd be able to see for myself whether the dolphin was still there.

That was what Nia would do. Or Julia, probably. Maybe even Amber if it was something she wanted badly enough.

I frowned, not wanting to think about my friends right now. Instead I stepped over to my desk and flipped open my laptop. Soon I was surfing the 'net, looking for information about dolphins.

More information, that was. I'd already memorized everything I could about my favorite animal. But that didn't mean I knew it all . . .

To my surprise, I quickly discovered something I hadn't known—this wasn't the first time a dolphin had swum into the Gowanus Canal. I gulped as I skimmed one of the articles I found. The last time it had happened, the poor dolphin hadn't survived . . .

I quickly clicked away from that, hoping that Dr. Hernandez and the others knew what they were doing. They wouldn't let my dolphin die, would they? She wasn't sick; just confused. Right?

For a few minutes I bounced around to different sites, though I seemed unable to focus on any of them. Then my attention caught on a headline that read "Dolphin Spotting in Montauk." Clicking on the link, I saw that it led to a blog article about a whale-and-dolphin-watching cruise out on Long

Island. The blogger was listed as John Dory and I smiled, recognizing that immediately as the name of a species of fish. Was it the blogger's real name? I doubted it, especially since the blog appeared to be all about marine biology and related subjects.

I skimmed the entry about the cruise— apparently the blogger hadn't seen any whales, but he had spotted some dolphins—and then scrolled down through the latest few posts. There was one about the SeaGlass Carousel in Manhattan and another that talked about recent upgrades at the aquarium right here in Brooklyn.

I wonder if John Dory is from New York City, I thought, scrolling back up to look for a photo of the blogger. But there wasn't one; instead, at the top of the page was a picture of a cool-looking puffer fish.

Oh well; it didn't really matter, I figured. For the next few minutes I looked around the blog some more, reading entries about a shark sighting at Rockaway Beach and seashell hunting at Sandy

Hook in New Jersey. Whoever this John Dory was, he seemed to know his stuff. I bookmarked the page so I could follow the blog after this.

Then I crawled into bed with the laptop, reading more until I couldn't stop yawning. Only then did I put the computer aside, snuggle under the covers, and try to push worries about my canal dolphin out of my head as I drifted off to sleep.

4

The next morning I woke up still thinking about the dolphin. So once I sat up and shoved a few stray strands of wavy hair out of my face, I grabbed my laptop off my bedside table and logged on.

I checked John Dory's blog first thing, even though I knew it was unlikely that it would have been updated in the past eight hours. But to my amazement, a new entry had been posted just twenty minutes ago!

"Dolphin Sighted in Gowanus Canal," the headline read.

My jaw dropped. How had the blogger found out about that? I skimmed the rest of the post:

On Monday afternoon, a solitary bottlenose dolphin was spotted by a Brooklyn resident in the Gowanus Canal near Ninth Street. Dolphins generally live in groups known as pods, so it's odd to see one on its own, especially in the canal, which New Yorkers know isn't welcoming to wildlife thanks to years of pollution. Local marine biologists have observed the dolphin and no illness or injury was evident. So for now, they watch and wait—and hope that the dolphin finds its way back out to sea.

A Brooklyn resident—that was me! But who had written this?

Maybe he works at the aquarium, I thought.

That made sense, actually. Several of the other entries had mentioned the aquarium, and most of the rest involved topics local to New York City and the surrounding area. What if Dr. Hernandez was John Dory? Or Dr. Gallagher, or Ms. Khan, or maybe someone like that water-quality tech I'd run into yesterday morning? Lots of people worked at the aquarium, and it was possible that any of them could have heard about the dolphin sighting. Maybe I could ask Eddy about it the next time I visited the aquarium, since he seemed to know everything about everyone there.

Or I could ask John Dory himself right now, I told myself, scrolling down to the comments section. There were no comments yet on this entry, and for a moment I stared at the little box, wondering if I had the guts to post my question there: Who are you?

My phone buzzed on the desk where I'd set it last night. Leaving the laptop where it was, I went over to see who was texting me. Probably just Julia or Amber, I figured, sending more stupid news about the stupid fun they were having at stupid summer camp . . .

But no. The text was from Olivia Choi! I hadn't even known she had my number.

Hi, Lily! the message read. **It was good to see you**

yesterday. A bunch of people are going roller-skating at the rink in Prospect Park tomorrow. Want to come? We're meeting at my place at 10:30.

I bit my lip, reading over the text again. I'd been skating at that rink a couple of times with Nia, and once with Julia and Amber, though we'd never gone back because Amber said the skates made her ankles hurt.

Still, I was pretty sure that even Amber would say yes to this invitation if Olivia Choi was the one asking. Then again, Amber wasn't here right now, and neither was Julia. If all three of us were going, I'd say yes in a heartbeat. But now? I stared at the words on the screen, not sure what to do. It was a relief when I heard Ozzy shouting down the hall that breakfast was ready. I clicked off my phone without responding to Olivia's text.

Twenty minutes later, I'd just about finished my eggs when Nia arrived to pick me up. "Hi, Giordanos," she greeted the whole family cheerfully. "What's shaking?"

"Not much," Ricky said, while my mother smiled and waved and Ozzy just grunted.

"Good morning, Nia." My father was already lacing up his work shoes. "How's Lily doing on her reading list? You keeping her focused?"

"Sure thing, Mr. G." Nia's tone was relaxed and friendly, even though my father had sounded kind of accusatory, at least in my opinion. "But it's no work at all for me to keep her focused. That girl loves to read."

"Hmph." Dad shot me a glance, then returned his attention to his shoes. "Let's go, boys," he added. "We've got a busy schedule today."

After they left, my mother offered Nia a cup of coffee, which she accepted. As she sat down to drink it, Mom disappeared into her room to get ready for work. Her shift at the MTA didn't start until nine, but she liked to arrive early.

When I heard the bedroom door click shut, I set down my fork. "Can we check on the dolphin on our way to the studio?" I asked Nia, keeping my voice low so there was no chance my mom would overhear. "It's right on the way, and I promise I'll start reading right after that, and—"

"Stop." She held up her hand. "I'm way ahead of you. I've been wondering how our fishy friend is doing myself."

"Dolphins aren't fish," I corrected her before I could stop myself. "They're mammals. They have to come to the surface to breathe, since they have lungs like people instead of gills like fish, and . . ."

This time I stopped talking when she started laughing. "Sorry, Marine Biolily," she said. "I knew that, okay? Just taking a little artistic license."

I smiled sheepishly. "Okay."

She sipped her coffee. "Actually, I thought about going back out there to check on the dolphin last night," she said. "But I got caught up finishing a couple of things and forgot. We'll go look as soon as I finish this, okay?"

Nia was as good as her word. Fifteen minutes

later, we were hurrying across the parking lot toward the canal. I headed straight for the inlet.

"Anybody out there?" I called, trying to sound lighthearted and not like I was dying with worry. Was she still there? If not, did it mean she'd found her way back to her pod? Or could something terrible have happened? And could I live with never knowing for sure?

At first I thought I was going to have to find out the answer to that last question, because the dirty water was still, broken only by a fast food wrapper floating near the mouth of the inlet. Nia joined me at the fence and did her best to perform the dolphin whistles I'd taught her the day before. I added my own chirps and grunts to that, but for a second I thought it wasn't going to do any good . . .

"There!" Nia exclaimed at last.

I squinted in the direction she was pointing. It was the dolphin! She was just poking her snout out of the water, but a second later she surfaced fully.

I let out a few whistles, and I was pretty sure she was listening. She even swam a little closer and stared at us for a few seconds, her dark eyes seeming to meet and hold mine. Then she dived down again out of sight.

"She looks okay!" I cried, relieved.

Nia nodded. "That's good news. But I guess she hasn't figured out how to get out of here yet, which is not-so-good news."

"Yeah." I chewed my lower lip. The joy I'd felt at seeing the dolphin again was fading fast, replaced by anxiety. "Maybe we should call the aquarium people and let them know she's still here."

Nia looked unconvinced. "They said they'd check back," she reminded me. "And they also said they wanted to give her a couple of days." Then she sighed, obviously reading the worry in my eyes. "But I guess it couldn't hurt to text them an update, right?"

"Right." I smiled. "Thanks."

Moments after Nia sent her text, her phone erupted in a ringtone that sounded like breaking glass. "It's a reply from Dr. Hernandez," she said.

"Let me see." When she handed me the phone, I scanned the text:

Thanks for the update. It's still too soon to give up hope that the dolphin will find her way home on her own. We received a report of a bottlenose pod being spotted in Upper New York Bay. We suspect this dolphin might have become separated from that pod. We don't want to take her away if she might still reunite with them.

"That makes sense, I guess," I murmured, reading over the last part again. The Gowanus Canal spilled out into the Upper New York Bay, also known as New York Harbor. If that was this dolphin's pod out there, they weren't that far away. So why didn't she try to find her way back to them?

"Come on." Nia plucked her phone out of my hand and tucked it in her pocket. "Let's get to the studio. I have work to do, and so do you." She winked. "I don't want to get in trouble with your daddy, right?"

I glanced out just in time to see the dolphin poke her head out of the water. She was still staring in our direction, almost as if she knew what we were saying and didn't want us to go. My heart ached with the wish to stay where I was, but I knew Nia was right. If my father knew we were here even now . . .

"Okay," I agreed with a sigh. "Let's go."

5

Nia's studio was just a few blocks away, surrounded by warehouses and wholesale businesses and stuff like that. At first I'd been surprised that she paid money every month to rent what was basically just a big room with cement floors and fluorescent lights that buzzed all the time like a hive of annoyed wasps. But then I'd visited her tiny apartment in Fort Greene, which she shared with three other people, and I got it. Compared to that place, the studio felt spacious and quiet. It used to be part of a factory, but it was hard to imagine that now, since Nia had hung paintings and tapestries on the bare walls and her sculptures stood all around the place—a clay statue of an old man near the door; a huge, swooping mixed-media owl hanging from the ceiling; and a giant metal block of Swiss cheese over by the tiny kitchen nook.

She'd also added a few pieces of furniture scavenged from the street. My favorite was the sofa, a once-grand Victorian piece covered in threadbare red velvet that I'd helped Nia patch with bits of brightly colored ribbon and old wool socks, turning it into a cheerful hodgepodge. I sat down there and dumped *The Call of the Wild* out of my bag while Nia stepped over to the large bin of spare metal pieces and other random junk that she called her Creativity Crate.

"What are you going to do for your next piece?" I asked, even though I wasn't really focused on that. "Penguins?"

"Nah." Nia poked at a scrap of corrugated roof, then pulled out a chunk of wood and studied it. "I'm not really feeling the penguin thing after all.

I think I'll just play with this stuff, see what it tells me it wants to be . . ."

I nodded, familiar with her process after several summers of watching her at work. For the next few days, she was likely to tinker and think, sticking random bits of stuff together and then pulling it apart again until she figured out what she wanted to create next.

It was usually fun to watch her in this creative groove. But this time, I wasn't feeling it. Mainly because she usually got so focused that she didn't want to do anything else until she settled on a subject, which meant no more trips to the aquarium for a while, or to visit the dolphin in the canal, either—at least not without a whole lot of begging.

Swallowing a sigh, I opened my book. Maybe if I read enough, Nia would want to reward me by taking me back to check on the dolphin. It seemed like my best bet, anyway . . .

I tried my best. I really did. But I couldn't seem

to focus on the story. I'd read the same sentence about six times without really taking it in when the buzz of my cell phone interrupted.

It was a text from Julia.

Wassup? So A and I snuck out last night. Went to the boys' cabin and made ghost noises outside. Soooo much fun! They cried like lil babies, haha! You shoulda seen it! This girl Chandra even got vid with her phone. Show you when we get back. Byyyye!

I clicked off the phone with a little more force than necessary. Why were they still sending me texts? I hadn't responded to any of them. Anyway, it sounded like they were having tons of fun with their new friends, like "this girl Chandra," whoever she was. So why were they taking time out of their busy schedules to pester me?

Glancing at Nia, I saw that she was bent over a small pile of metal and wood, moving a tangle of wire back and forth every few seconds. Apparently she hadn't even heard my phone go off. That was no huge surprise. When she was this focused, I could probably do a handstand and she wouldn't notice.

Or I could sneak out and visit the dolphin, I thought.

My heart immediately started thumping at the very thought. Sneak out? Me? No way. I never did anything disobedient or daring. Wasn't that what Julia was always telling me?

I opened my book again, staring at the page without really seeing it. What if I did it, though? All I had to do was wander over toward the studio door and see what happened. If Nia looked up and caught me, I could pretend I was heading for the tiny bathroom tucked into the alcove near the entryway.

And if she didn't catch me . . . I closed my eyes, thinking about the way the dolphin had stared at me earlier. As if she knew I cared, that I was there to make sure she was okay.

With my eyes closed, all I could see was the dolphin swimming around in my mind. I had to see her. I wasn't sure why; I just did.

I opened my eyes and stood up, tucking my phone in my pocket and leaving my book and other stuff on the sofa. Then I strolled toward the front part of the studio, doing my best to look casual. I peeked at Nia, who was still hunched over her work with her back to me. My heart was pounding so loudly that I couldn't believe she didn't hear it. Five more steps to the door, four, three, two . . . Before I knew it, I was carefully sliding back the dead bolt, then easing the door open and shut again . . .

Outside, I collapsed against the rough brick wall and gulped in several lungfuls of steamy summer air. I definitely wasn't cut out for a life of crime. Still, I'd already broken the rules—I might as well take advantage. I would just dash over to the canal and check on the dolphin, then come right back again. With any luck, I could sneak in without Nia ever realizing I was gone.

I half walked, half ran the whole way to the canal. As I crossed the parking lot, I could see someone else in the little grassy area near the inlet. It was a young woman with a stroller. When I got closer, I saw a toddler clinging to the fence staring out at the water.

The woman heard me coming and turned quickly. But when she saw me, she relaxed and returned her attention to the child.

The toddler turned around, his face smeared with red and blue and yellow goo. I guessed it had come from the enormous lollipop he was clutching in one hand. "Fishy!" he shouted. "Mama, fishy fishy!"

"Yes, fishy." The woman wandered closer. "Oh look, there really is a fishy out there!"

They were looking at the dolphin. When I came closer, I saw her, too. She was floating at the surface not far from the edge, watching the toddler with what looked like curiosity.

"Fishy!" the little boy shouted again.

With effort, I managed not to correct him. Instead I watched the dolphin as she sank under the water for a moment, then reemerged a little closer.

Catching a glimpse of motion out of the corner of my eye, I turned just in time to see the toddler raise his hand. "Candy for fishy!" he cried with glee.

"No!" I blurted out.

He froze and stared at me, astonished. "What did you say to him?" The mother hurried over and put a protective hand on her son's head.

"He, uh, looked like he was going to throw that in." I gestured to the lollipop. "If the dolphin eats something like that, it could make her sick."

The young woman just glared at me for a moment, as if I'd accused her son of trying to murder someone. "Whatever," she spat out at last. "Come on, kiddo. It's too hot to stay out here anyway."

She grabbed the kid and shoved him in the stroller, ignoring his howls of protest. The lollipop ended up on the grass, sticky and dirty and gross. I shuddered, glad that the kid hadn't thrown it at the dolphin. Maybe she wouldn't have eaten it, but I didn't want to take any chances.

"Hey, girl," I called softly as soon as the young mother and her son had disappeared. "How's it going?"

The dolphin was still floating at the surface. She chirped, then dived down out of sight for a moment. But she soon returned, seeming to smile at me as she lifted her head out of the water.

I smiled back. She was so beautiful! The grimy canal faded away and I imagined her with her pod, leaping and skimming over the waves . . .

Then I looked around, the dingy surroundings coming back into focus. What if someone else came along and threw something in the water like that kid had tried to? I thought back to Zach and his friends tossing gravel. There were too many stupid or mean people around who might do just about anything.

I knew I needed to get back to the studio. But I

couldn't. Not yet. I had to stay and make sure the dolphin was safe.

"Nia will freak out whenever she finally notices I'm gone," I said, sinking down onto the grass by the fence. "But whatever. I'll take my punishment. It's worth it to help you."

The dolphin was still floating there, watching me. She let out a soft chirp, almost as if she were responding to what I'd just said.

"My name's Lily, by the way," I told her with a little wave. "I wonder what your name is."

With a sharp whistle, the dolphin dived down again. She stayed underwater for a couple of minutes—so long that I was starting to wonder if she was going to return. What if she'd finally figured out how to leave the canal? I decided that if she didn't surface in the next five minutes, I would go back to Nia's studio and see if I could still sneak in without being caught.

Pulling out my phone, I checked the time.

Three minutes passed, then another fifteen seconds, and another ten . . .

And then she was there, splashing out of the water in what was almost a jump, then rolling over. I smiled, both happy to see her and sad that she was still stuck in this dirty canal.

"I guess you must like it here in the Gowanus," I told her with a wry smile. "Maybe that's what I should call you—Gowanus Girl."

I rolled that name around in my mind for a moment. But somehow, it felt too harsh for the beautiful dolphin. Like too much of a mouthful.

"Gowanus," I murmured thoughtfully. "What's short for Gowanus? Gowy? Nussy? Wanny?" Suddenly an idea struck me. "No, not Wanny—Wanda!"

I smiled, liking the name. The dolphin was watching me again.

"What do you think?" I asked her. "Is your name Wanda?"

She chirped and swam a little closer. That settled it! Wanda it was!

For the next half hour, I talked to Wanda whenever she was at the surface. Eventually I noticed that she was coming closer and closer to the edge where I was sitting. Almost close enough to touch . . .

I sat up and looked around. Most of the cars were at the other end of the parking lot near the store. That was way too far away for anyone to notice what I was doing, especially behind the partial shelter of the picnic tables, benches, and spindly trees dotting the grassy area.

Still, I felt guilty and devious as I clambered awkwardly over the fence. It seemed strange to be on the other side, with nothing between me and the murky water. But I ignored that and crouched down, hanging on to the fence with one hand as I waited for Wanda to surface again.

When she did, the dolphin seemed surprised to see me so close. At least that was what I read in her dark eyes. Still, she didn't move, floating where she was.

"Hey, Wanda," I said softly. "Is it okay if I . . .?"

I stretched out my arm, reaching toward her snout. My fingers came within inches of the smooth gray skin before the dolphin dodged away, disappearing quickly underwater.

"Too fast," I chided myself in a whisper. "You scared her."

I waited for her to surface again. After a moment she did, though she was farther away this time.

"It's okay, Wanda," I called in a singsong voice. "It's just me, your friend Lily." I gave a few whistles and chirps for good measure. "Sorry I scared you. I don't blame you for being wary of people." I sighed, leaning back against the fence. "Actually, I kind of feel that way myself lately. It's like I can't even trust the people I thought I knew best. Like I don't quite fit in my own life anymore sometimes, or . . ."

"Hey!" a voice called from somewhere behind me.

I was so startled I almost fell into the canal. "N-Nia!" I stammered, my face instantly going red.

Sure enough, Nia was striding toward me across the grass. I quickly climbed back over the fence, bracing myself for whatever came next.

6

When Nia reached me, she was frowning. "I figured I'd find you here, sneaky girl," she said.

"I'm sorry," I said, looking down at my feet, not quite ready to meet Nia's fierce dark eyes. "I'm really sorry, seriously, Nia! I was so worried about Wanda, and I just had to come check on her again, and it's a good thing I did, too—some little kid was about to throw his lollipop at her, and I was afraid someone else might come along and harass her, or . . ."

"Chill," Nia broke in with a little half smile. "You don't have to explain. I get it."

"You do?" I gulped and shot her a sidelong glance, still not quite daring to believe I wasn't in deep, dark trouble. "I mean, okay, but I know it was wrong and stuff. If my dad knew, he'd blow a gasket."

"Yeah." She shrugged. "But he doesn't know. And I'm not your dad, right?"

I finally met her eyes. She didn't look as angry as I'd expected.

"You—you're not mad?" I asked. "I thought you'd want to kill me."

"Only a little," she said. "Actually, I'm kind of proud of you, Lilykins."

"Proud?" That didn't compute at all. "Why?"

Nia shrugged. "You rebelled against authority for something you believe in. That's pretty cool as far as I'm concerned." She winked. "Even if I have to play the role of authority in this scenario, which so isn't me, okay?"

"Okay," I said slowly, still trying to catch up. "But if my dad finds out . . ."

"He won't. Not unless you decide to tell him."
Nia crooked her finger at me. "Now come on, let's
go back to the studio."

"Oh. Um, okay." My heart sank as I imagined
the whole rest of the day spent sitting on the hodgepodge sofa chafing to know what was going on
with Wanda.

But as it turned out, Nia had something different in mind. When we reached the studio she went
flying around, stuffing things into her backpack—
a sketchpad, a bunch of pencils, a big floppy sun hat.

"See if those beach chairs are still in the
storage loft," she instructed me.

A bit mystified—was she planning to incorpo-
rate the beach chairs into her next sculpture?—I
obeyed, climbing up the wooden ladder built
against one wall and crawling into the space over
the bathroom where Nia tossed anything she wasn't
likely to need anytime soon.

"Is this it?" I called, poking my head out along
with part of a rickety folding chair.

"There should be two. Toss them down—and the beach umbrella, too, if the moths haven't eaten it."

Once again, I did as she said. When I climbed back down, she was over at the kitchenette making peanut butter sandwiches.

"What are you doing?" I said. "It's kind of early for lunch, isn't it?"

"Yes, but we'll be hungry soon enough." She tucked the sandwiches into a plastic pouch. "Bring your books, too. If we're going to camp out in that parking lot for the next day or two, you can at least get some of your reading done."

I gasped, finally catching on. "We're going back to watch over Wanda?" I cried.

"Wanda?"

"That's what I decided to call her." I quickly explained how I'd come up with the name. "Thanks, Nia!"

"No worries." Nia strode back over and added the food to her backpack. "I'm not having much luck coming up with ideas today anyway. Maybe if I sketch that crazy dolphin again it'll inspire something."

I couldn't resist grabbing her in a big hug. "I mean it," I said, my words slightly muffled by the voluminous patchwork poncho she was wearing. "Thanks, Nia. You're the best."

When we arrived back at the canal, the first thing I did was check for Wanda, who surfaced almost immediately. Then Nia and I set up the beach chairs on the grass by the inlet. The umbrella turned out to be too full of holes to be any use against the sun, so Nia called one of her roommates, who turned up a short while later with a boom box and a crazy pink feathered parasol.

"So where's this dolphin?" The roommate's name was Wallace, but everyone called him Inky because of the tattoos that covered nearly every inch of him. I stared at the one of a swordfish on his arm, mesmerized by the way it moved and flexed with his muscles.

"Over there." Nia looked up and nodded toward the inlet. She was perched on one of the beach chairs sketching away and sipping one of the sodas she'd brought.

Inky wandered over, and a second later Wanda surfaced. "Whoa!" he exclaimed. "There really is a dolphin in there!"

I didn't hear whatever Nia said in response. Several people were coming toward us from the parking lot—a woman and two men, all of them appearing to be in their late twenties.

"Hey, is this a party or what?" one of the men asked when they reached us.

"Private party, sorry," Nia said with her easy smile. "But here—have a cookie."

She offered up a box of Oreos she must have stuck in the backpack when I wasn't looking. The men eagerly helped themselves, but their friend was peering at the canal.

"Hey, what's out there?" she asked. "Is that a dolphin?"

"No way!" Soon all three of them were at the fence with Inky, who started proudly explaining about Wanda.

I glanced at Nia, a little worried. We were supposed to be protecting the dolphin. And so far, all we seemed to be doing was drawing more attention to her.

Nia was busy with the boom box, fiddling with the dials until she found a station she liked. "There," she said with a smile, turning up the volume. "*Now* it's a party."

The rest of the afternoon went pretty much the same way. People came over to us, drawn by the music or the sight of the pink parasol or whatever. Some of them noticed the dolphin, some didn't. Nia had to stop one guy from trying to feed part of his doughnut to Wanda, and an old man made a few jokes about how she looked like a big seafood dinner, but most of the people were pretty nice.

I was sitting by the fence in my beach chair, reading my book, when I heard a clang from nearby. It was Nia dragging a mangled metal car bumper toward our spot.

"What's that?" I set down my book and stood up to stretch my legs.

"Isn't it cool? I just found it in the parking lot." She beamed down at the bumper, which she'd dropped on the grass next to a dented bleach bottle, a broken flowerpot, and an old hubcap. "I think it's going to become my dolphin's tail."

"Huh?" Then I caught on. "Wait—you decided to do a dolphin sculpture?"

"Why not? Wanda inspired me." Nia grinned at me, and then at Wanda. "Every time I start to sketch something else, it turns into a dolphin. I figure I'll get started right away. There's tons of stuff lying around here that I can use, and I can always look for more over there." She waved a hand toward Ninth Street, where there was a big outdoor shop full of used furniture, old window frames, and all kinds of other stuff.

"Cool," I said, though I was distracted. I'd just spotted Dani Levitski, a girl from my class at school, coming toward us with her mother. They were both holding shopping bags from the hardware store.

"Hey, Lily, it really is you!" Dani beamed at me and pushed her glasses up her nose. "I heard about your dolphin."

"You did? Where?"

"My sister's boyfriend was here this morning," Dani said. "He saw the dolphin. So where is it?"

I had no idea which of our visitors was Dani's sister's boyfriend, and I didn't really care. Dani was already rushing toward the fence, and I followed.

"Hurry up, Dani." Her mother checked her watch. "We have more errands."

Dani ignored her, clinging to the fence and staring at Wanda. "It's so cool!" she exclaimed. "A real live dolphin."

Her voice was kind of shrieky, and it seemed to startle Wanda. The dolphin burst into motion and dived down out of view.

"Oh, she's gorgeous, isn't she?" Dani cried, not seeming to notice that she'd scared Wanda away. "How'd she end up here, anyway?"

I forced a smile. I was getting kind of tired of explaining things to everyone who stopped by. Still, I knew it was only natural. It wasn't every day that a dolphin showed up in Brooklyn.

"We think she just got lost," I said. "We're hoping she decides to rejoin her pod soon. That's the group of dolphins she lives with—dolphins are really social animals, and—"

"That's enough, Dani," Mrs. Levitski called out, interrupting me. "We have to go."

"Sorry." Dani shot me a quick smile. "Hey, are you going skating tomorrow? Olivia invited you, right? She said she did."

I was surprised to hear that Olivia Choi was talking about me. "Um, I'm not sure yet," I told

Dani. "It sort of depends on, you know . . ." I waved a hand toward the spot where Wanda had disappeared.

"Dani!" Mrs. Levitski's voice was sharper. "Now."

"Bye," Dani said to me, and then rushed off.

I collapsed back in my chair. Nia was fiddling with the bleach bottle and the hubcap, trying to figure out how to wedge them together. "Your friend seemed nice," she commented absently.

"She's not really my friend," I said, standing up and walking over for a better look at what Nia was doing. "Just a girl I know."

Nia looked up, her expression puzzled. Before she could say anything, she widened her eyes at something behind me. "Whoa," she said. "Looks like we made the news!"

I looked over my shoulder. A van sporting the logo of one of the local TV stations had just pulled into a parking spot nearby. Two people climbed out—a pudgy, sweaty man in a loose linen shirt and a pretty woman I recognized from the evening news. She was the one who reported on interesting local stories in Brooklyn and Queens.

"We heard about the dolphin," the man announced. "Can we get some footage?"

"Sure," Nia said. "She's right over there. Her name's Wanda. And this is Lily—she's the one who found her."

"Really?" The reporter looked at me with interest.

"I don't want to be on TV," I said, taking a quick step backward. I could only imagine what my parents would say if they turned on the TV tonight and saw me hanging out by the canal!

The woman shrugged. "Fine. We should interview someone, though." She glanced back toward Nia. "Want to say a few words?"

"Sure, if you let me mention my art," Nia said with a smile. "A girl's gotta eat, right?"

The man chuckled. "Whatever." He gestured to whoever was still in the van. "Let's set up!" he called.

I watched from the fence as the news crew bustled around with cameras and microphones. A woman was touching up the reporter's makeup when a shout came from the parking lot.

"What's going on out here?" It was a middle-aged man wearing a short-sleeved button-down shirt and a striped tie. He marched up to us, glaring around at everyone. "This is private property, you know."

"Uh-oh," I murmured.

I'd thought I was saying it to myself, but the man heard me. He frowned briefly at me, taking in the beach chairs and parasol. Then he turned toward Nia and the news crew and started blustering at them. It turned out he was the assistant manager of the hardware store.

I stayed quiet, watching Wanda as she appeared and disappeared in the inlet. What if the assistant manager kicked us out? I wouldn't be able to check on Wanda anymore. Maybe he wouldn't even let the scientists come back to help her!

But I tried not to panic. Nia was already giving the man her most charming smile, the one that almost always got us free extra scoops at the ice cream place or a bonus round at the bowling alley. And the news reporter was helping, too, telling the manager how much good publicity their story would bring to his store.

In the end, the manager stood in the background while the woman did her report about Wanda. I stayed well out of camera range myself, holding my breath until they all went away and I could relax and watch Wanda again in peace.

Our second day by the canal started out a little quieter. It was hot and humid, and not many people came into the parking lot. We probably only had a half dozen visitors by lunchtime, including the assistant manager, who was acting much nicer today. He even brought us cold bottles of water from the store.

"I guess he liked the way he looked on TV," Nia whispered with a mischievous little smile as the man hurried away.

I stifled a laugh. I'd seen the report about Wanda on the five o'clock news, though luckily nobody else in my family had caught it. My mother had still been at work, my dad had been in the shower, and my brothers had been in the kitchen arguing about what to have for dinner. My secret was safe—at least until someone who had seen the story mentioned it to some member of my family . . .

But I was trying not to worry about that. Why borrow trouble? That was what Nia always said. Maybe she was right. Worrying had never stopped bad stuff from happening before, so what was the point?

After lunch, a few more people started showing up. Most of them mentioned seeing the story about Wanda on the news or reading about it online that morning on the TV station's website or on social media. A few headed into the hardware store after visiting Wanda, which I guessed would make the assistant manager happy.

Meanwhile Nia's sculpture was starting to take shape. She'd brought an armature along from the studio that morning. That was a wire frame on a wooden base—she built most of her sculptures on a similar structure. She'd been busy bending the wire into the right shape and then attaching stuff to it all day.

"It's looking good so far," I commented as I watched her fiddle with it. "It's actually starting to look like a dolphin!"

"Don't sound so surprised." Nia grinned at me, then eyed the sculpture and pulled off a wad of sparkly fabric she'd just attached. "I'm liking the direction it's going."

I watched for another moment or two, then wandered back to the fence to check on Wanda. The dolphin surfaced as soon as I whistled for her, and I smiled. Lately it seemed as if she was getting attuned to me. Or was that my imagination?

"No, it's true," I whispered, not wanting even Nia to overhear. "We're becoming friends, right?"

Wanda chirped and swam a little closer. I was thinking about trying to touch her again when I heard a commotion from the parking lot.

When I turned around, I saw more than a dozen kids my age coming toward us. In the lead was Olivia Choi. She had a pair of roller skates slung around her neck by the laces and a big smile on her face.

"Hi, Lily!" she greeted me when she got close enough. "Dani said you'd probably be here."

Dani Levitski materialized out of the group. "Yeah, I told them I saw you," she announced proudly. "And that you might be too busy to come skating."

"Sorry you missed it, though." Olivia played with the loose end of her skate laces. "We had fun. Maybe you can come next time."

"Maybe," I said cautiously.

Most of the other kids were heading for the fence, jostling one another and chattering and laughing as they all looked for Wanda. But a girl named Chloe Darrow stayed behind with Olivia, Dani, and me. Chloe was the type of person who always wanted to know everything about everybody else.

"So when do Julia and Amber come back from soccer camp?" Chloe asked me in her nasal, always slightly too loud voice. "You must really miss them, huh? You guys do, like, everything together."

"Um . . ." I wasn't sure what to say. Olivia and Dani were watching me, waiting for my response.

"Hey, there it is!" a girl shouted from over by the water.

Whew! Wanda had just surfaced, and now everybody wanted a look at her—including Olivia, Dani, and Chloe. The three of them dashed over to join the others, completely forgetting about me.

And I was glad. I just didn't know how to respond to questions about Julia and Amber.

About my so-called best friends, who had totally betrayed me . . .

I'd been trying not to think about them. But now it all came rushing back. How they'd begged me to go to sleepaway camp with them, even though I wanted to go to this marine biology camp in Maine I'd heard about. But no, regular camp would be fun, they said. A month of toasting marshmallows, canoeing, arts and crafts, exploring the woods upstate, learning archery, stuff like that. Fun, fun, fun.

And it *had* sounded like fun. I'd even talked my parents into paying for it, and they'd sent a deposit.

But then Julia heard about a sleepaway soccer camp that was running at the same time. She and Amber decided they'd rather do that, and they'd gone ahead and registered without even discussing it with me. Oh, they'd told me about it afterward, of course, acting as if they assumed I would want to switch, too. Even though they knew I didn't like soccer, or have much interest in any sports. Even though they always made fun of me in gym class when I accidentally kicked the ball the wrong way . . .

I gritted my teeth, going hot and cold with anger all over again. The worst part had been telling my parents. My dad had grumbled about wasting the deposit money, and my mom had just given me a sad look, as if she knew exactly what had happened even though I hadn't told them the whole story.

I hadn't told Julia and Amber the whole story, either, actually. I'd just said that my dad had changed his mind, that his work truck needed repairs and so he couldn't pay for camp this year after all. Somehow it had seemed even more painful to admit how much they'd hurt me—

"This is so cool!" Olivia Choi walked over to me, phone in hand. Before I could move, she raised it and snapped a couple of photos of me. "I can't believe there's really a dolphin here." She fiddled with her phone, peering at the screen. "There! I just posted some of my pictures." She smiled. "And I gave you credit for spotting the dolphin, too."

I gulped. Olivia was so popular—I could only imagine how many people would see whatever she posted on social media. What if Julia and Amber saw it? What would they think?

Worse yet, what if my brothers saw it? They might tell my parents, and then I'd be in real trouble.

It was getting harder and harder not to worry, not to borrow trouble. I did my best to smile and act normal as Olivia and the others said good-bye and left.

Nia had been mostly ignoring my classmates and working on her sculpture. But she looked up once we were alone again.

"Those kids seemed nice," she said.

"Yeah, I guess." I walked over to check on Wanda. This time when I whistled, it took several seconds before she appeared. Even then, she didn't really look at me.

Nia joined me at the fence. "She looks a little listless," she said. "I hope she's not getting sick from being in that dirty water."

"Yeah." Fear stabbed through me as she put my worry into words. "Should we call the aquarium people?"

Nia pulled out her phone. "Well, it hasn't been two full days yet," she said. "But I guess it couldn't hurt to send a quick text."

Two hours later, I was helping Nia hoist her half-finished sculpture onto a handcart so we could take it back to the studio when a car pulled up to the edge of the lot. Dr. Gallagher, the female scientist from the other day, climbed out.

"Hi there," she greeted us, though her gaze was already moving toward the water. "So is she still here?"

"Uh-huh." I glanced over at Wanda, who was floating at the surface. "She's acting kind of, I don't know, tired or something. We're afraid she might be sick after all."

The scientist watched the dolphin for a moment in silence. Finally she nodded, pulled out her phone, and tapped in a quick text.

"Okay," she said to Nia and me after that. "We'll move her to the aquarium in the morning."

7

When Nia and I arrived the next morning, we found the half of the parking lot nearer the canal blocked off by police barricades. A crowd of curious onlookers had already gathered nearby. We pushed our way through them.

"Sorry, young ladies," the police officer guarding the gate told us. "Nobody can go past this point."

"But we're with the aquarium people," Nia argued.

The officer shook his head. "I don't think so."

While Nia continued to argue and cajole, I stood on tiptoes, trying to see what was going on.

But my view was mostly blocked by a large flatbed truck containing a huge metal crate. Another truck with a crane on the back was parked nearby, along with several other vehicles.

I bet they're going to transport Wanda in that box, I thought, staring at the crate. *She's probably going to be terrified . . .*

"Please," I begged. "We have to get through. Wanda needs me!"

"Wanda?" The police officer scratched his neck. "Who's that?"

"Never mind." Nia tugged on my arm, pulling me away. "Hold that thought," she told me. "I'm calling Dr. Hernandez."

I crossed my fingers behind my back as Nia made the call. She had to do a little more cajoling, but when she hung up she was smiling.

"Is he letting us in?" I asked.

"Uh-huh." She headed for the barricade again. "Come on, we just have to wait until he gets here."

That didn't take long. Moments later Dr. Hernandez was ushering us past the police.

"I probably shouldn't let you in," he told us with a rueful smile. "But since you're the ones who found her . . ."

"Thanks, doc," Nia said. "It means a lot to Lily."

The scientist nodded at me. "You'll have to stay out of the way, all right?" he said. "This kind of transport is always tricky."

"How will you get her on the truck?" I asked. Over by the water, I could see several people in wet suits, and lots of others milling around wearing regular clothes.

"We'll have to herd her onto a sling." Dr. Hernandez pointed to a piece of fabric hanging from the crane. "It's specially designed for dolphins—there are cutouts for the flippers, see? Once she's in there, we'll lift her into the crate. Then several people will ride on the edge, keeping her moist and making sure she stays calm."

"There's no water in the crate?" I was surprised. "But she's used to being in the sea!"

He nodded. "If we were going farther, we'd have to do a wet transport," he said. "But since we're only going a short distance, this way is easier—we call it a moist transport."

I bit my lip and nodded, trying not to worry. "It might help to whistle to her along the way," I told him. "She seems to like that when I do it."

"Thanks for the suggestion." Dr. Hernandez smiled, but his gaze was drifting off over my shoulder toward the people by the inlet. "Why don't you watch from that bench over there?" With that, he hurried away.

"Come on." Nia took my hand and pulled me toward the bench. "We'd better stay out of the way, or we'll get kicked out."

But I couldn't sit still. Instead I stood in front of the bench, watching as the aquarium crew got started. First the wet-suit people lowered themselves into the canal and blocked the end of the inlet with a big net.

"Ew," Nia commented. "There's not a shower hot enough to wash off the stink of a swim in the Gowanus."

I knew she was joking, but I couldn't manage more than a weak half smile. I'd just spotted Wanda—she was in the far corner of the inlet, popping up and then diving down again repeatedly.

"She's already agitated," I said. "They need to let her calm down."

"Chill out." Nia kicked me lightly in the leg. "These people are experts, okay? They know how to do this."

I certainly hoped so. The problem was, nobody had told Wanda that. The dolphin continued to swim around restlessly as the crane started up and moved to the edge of the water. The operator lowered the arm, and the swimmers reached up to pull the sling underwater.

"How are they going to get her to swim into that thing?" I wondered aloud, my throat tight with anxiety. "She doesn't even want to get near them!"

Sure enough, every time one group of swimmers tried to herd her toward the ones holding the sling open, Wanda dived down or darted away. Finally I couldn't stand it anymore.

"I have to help," I exclaimed, hurrying forward.

"Lily! Stop! Where are you going?" Nia sounded startled, but I ignored her calls. She was the one who was so excited about resisting authority when you really believed in something, right? Well, that was what I was doing.

The aquarium people didn't seem to notice me creeping toward the edge of the inlet. I crouched down behind the fence at the end, clutching the metal bars.

Wanda was a couple of yards away. Three swimmers were moving slowly toward her, talking softly to one another. The dolphin was watching them warily; I could tell she was about to dive again . . .

"Wanda, it's me!" I called softly. Then I let out a few chirps and whistles.

The dolphin's eyes turned in my direction. She let out an uncertain chirp.

"Now!" one of the swimmers said.

The three of them moved forward. Wanda had been looking at me and was caught by surprise. She turned to dart away—and ended up swimming right into the sling!

"Got her!" one of the swimmers cried.

Before either Wanda or I knew what was happening, the sling was rising out of the water. All I could see of Wanda were her flippers and flukes flapping helplessly in the air. I gulped, and then let out another whistle, hoping she could hear it.

Moments later the sling had been lowered into the crate on the flatbed and I couldn't see her at all anymore. Several aquarium people scrambled up onto the edge of the crate, while others handed them sprayers. Dr. Hernandez and Dr. Gallagher were talking to the truck driver.

I hurried over to them. "I want to help," I said breathlessly. "Wanda—the dolphin—she knows me. I could sit up there with them, talk to her . . ." I waved a hand up toward the people on the crate.

Dr. Gallagher's eyebrows shot up in surprise. "What are you doing here?" she asked. "Never mind, I don't really want to know." She shot Dr. Hernandez a suspicious look. "In any case, it's out of the question. I'm sorry, but only trained personnel can ride with us."

"Sorry," Dr. Hernandez said. "Don't worry, Lily. I'll text your friend once Wanda is safely settled at the aquarium."

That wasn't good enough. I'd found Wanda; I'd helped get her into the sling, even if nobody had noticed. I had to be there when they unloaded her! What if she panicked, and I could have helped prevent it?

"But she needs me!" My voice came out louder than intended, and maybe a little squeakier, too. "Please," I added more softly. "I want to help."

Dr. Hernandez looked sympathetic. "Trust me, Lily, you've already helped this dolphin. I promise."

"Hey, boss!" one of the people on the crate called. "We going to get moving soon here? She's not happy."

"Right now!" Dr. Hernandez called back. Gesturing to the truck driver, he turned away and hurried off toward one of the cars parked nearby.

I gritted my teeth, feeling helpless. Maybe I could stow away; grab the bumper of the truck when it pulled out . . .

I wasn't sure if Nia had actually read my mind, but she appeared and grabbed me. "Don't worry," she said, dragging me out of the way as the flatbed truck roared to life. "I just spotted my buddy Basim in the crowd out there. He's got a car."

At first I had no idea what she was talking about. But fifteen minutes later we were several blocks away piling into a beat-up sedan with a tall guy around Nia's age sporting a Mohawk and a nose ring.

"This is so cool," Basim exclaimed. "A real dolphin here in Brooklyn? I never know what's going to happen when I run into you, Nia."

"That's what everyone says," I told him.

He laughed, glancing at me in the cracked rear-view mirror. "Seat belt on, Lily, please," he said. "You might have to dig down behind the seat to find it."

"It's worth it," Nia informed me. "Basim drives like a maniac."

That didn't turn out to be entirely true, though he did drive pretty fast. Still, we made it all the way to Coney Island in one piece. Basim dropped us off in front of the aquarium, wishing us luck.

"Need me to hang around and drive you back?" he offered.

"Thanks, we're good." Nia gave him a quick fist bump as she slid out of her front seat. "We can catch the train back."

"Thanks for the ride!" I added.

He tossed me a grinning salute, then took off in a cloud of exhaust. Meanwhile I'd just spotted the flatbed truck, now parked in the aquarium lot.

"Looks like they already unloaded her," Nia commented. "That was fast."

I guessed the delay in walking over to Basim's car had caused us to miss the truck's arrival. "Let's go," I said. "Maybe they'll let us see her."

When we got inside, Nia peeled off to use the restroom. "I'll find you in a bit," she told me. "Go see if you can talk your way backstage."

I knew exactly where to find the door that connected the public part of the aquarium and the private part—the labs and offices and holding tanks that Nia had referred to as "backstage." I'd seen various employees pass through that door a zillion times over the years. But I'd never been through it myself.

I stood a few feet away from it, staring at the EMPLOYEES ONLY sign. What would it hurt to knock on that door? The worst they could say was no . . .

Even so, I didn't quite dare. I just hovered there, waiting for Nia to arrive and do the scary part for me.

But then the door opened. Dr. Hernandez stepped out, wearing a white lab coat. He spotted me immediately.

"Lily!" He sounded surprised. "How did you get here?" His serious face twisted into a slight smile. "Did you stow away on the truck?"

"I thought about it," I said before I could stop myself. Then I cleared my throat. "Um, I mean, no. Nia's friend drove us. I was hoping, uh, that is, I thought maybe . . ." My tongue was getting all twisted up over the words. What was wrong with me?

But Dr. Hernandez was still smiling. "Why don't you come back and see Wanda?" he said. "We just got her settled in her temporary tank."

"Really?" I could hardly believe it. "Thank you! I mean, yes, sure, I'd love to!"

He held open the door, and I stepped through. "Backstage" wasn't very exciting at first—just a boring hallway. But I followed Dr. Hernandez through another door, and found myself in the main lab.

It was awesome! There were workers in lab coats, scientific equipment everywhere I looked, and lots of tanks of coral, fish, and other interesting creatures, though I was too distracted to look very closely. Because a huge glass tank was built into the far wall of the enormous main space, and Wanda was swimming around inside it!

"Go on and say hi." Dr. Hernandez checked his watch. "I'll be back shortly if you have any questions."

"Thanks," I said absently, barely aware that he was turning back toward the exit.

I walked over to the tank, eyes fixed on Wanda. She was moving slowly, looking a little confused. But for the first time, now that she was in the clear water of the tank instead of the murky Gowanus, I could see every inch of her. And she was beautiful!

"Hi, gorgeous," I murmured, putting my hand to the glass as the dolphin swam by. The top of the tank was a couple of yards above my head, with scaffolding leading up to a metal mesh platform that ran along the edge. I guessed that was where the workers went to feed or observe the creatures in the tank. Would I get in trouble if I climbed up there so I could look down and talk to her?

Before I could decide, I saw out of the corner of my eye that someone was striding toward me. Uh-oh—it was Susan, the water-quality tech I'd encountered before!

"Who are you, and what are you doing in here?" she demanded.

I was glad that she didn't seem to remember me. Still, she didn't look any friendlier than she had the last time I'd seen her.

"Um, Dr. Hernandez brought me?" I said uncertainly. I glanced around, hoping the scientist might have returned, but there was no sign of him. I didn't see Dr. Gallagher, either. "He said I could say hi to Wanda."

"Wanda? Who's that?"

"That's what I call the dolphin." I waved a hand toward the tank. "I'm the one who discovered her."

"Hmph." She narrowed her eyes at me. "I'll have to check with Dr. Hernandez."

She stalked off. I barely had time to heave a sigh of relief when someone else hurried toward me. To my surprise, I realized I recognized him, too. It was the boy who'd spoken to me at the walrus exhibit! The one Eddy had said was a student intern here.

"Hi," he said with a shy smile. "Sorry about Ms. Butler—she's always kind of cranky." He shot a quick look around, as if making sure that the water tech hadn't come back when he wasn't looking. "So are you the girl who found the dolphin? I saw you come in with my dad just now, so I figured . . ."

"You mean Dr. Hernandez? He's your dad?" That made sense. Eddy had told me that the boy's father was a scientist here.

"Uh-huh. I'm John Hernandez." He smiled. "What's your name?"

"Lily Giordano." I felt awkward, as if we should shake hands or something. But John kept his hands in his pockets, so I just folded mine across my chest. "And yeah, I'm the one who spotted Wanda."

"Wanda?" He tilted his head to one side, like a quizzical parrot or something.

"That's what I call her." I waved a hand toward the dolphin, then quickly explained how I'd come up with the name.

"Cool," he said with a laugh when I finished. "Wanda. I like it." He glanced over at her, and his smile faded slightly. "I just wish my dad had let me come along on the transport. I really would have liked to—Wait," he interrupted himself. "Were you there? Did you see it?"

"Yeah," I said. "I was there."

"Cool! So can I interview you for my blog? I want to write a follow-up about Wanda."

"You have a blog?" I flashed back to the one I'd just discovered. "Wait—you're not John Dory, are you?"

He looked startled. "How did you—you've seen my blog?"

"Yeah, I just started reading it." I stared at him, trying to reconcile the ordinary-looking kid standing in front of me with the cool articles I'd read. "I never would have guessed it was written by a kid!"

"Thanks." He grinned. "So does that mean I can interview you?"

I gulped, feeling a little trapped. It was bad enough that half of Brooklyn had probably already posted photos of me and Wanda on social media, and that Nia had been on TV talking about the dolphin. The last thing I needed was my name and face on a blog that anyone might stumble across!

"Uh, I don't think so," I said. "Sorry. I just don't . . . um . . ."

"Oh." John looked disappointed. "It's okay if you're too shy or whatever. I just thought . . ."

Suddenly everything felt awkward. I searched my mind for something to say, but all I could do was turn and stare at Wanda, who was floating in the middle of her tank.

"So . . ." John began.

"John!" Suddenly his father appeared, arms loaded with buckets. "A little help, please?"

"Coming!" John shot me an apologetic glance, then hurried toward Dr. Hernandez. I watched him go, envy coiling through me like an eel through coral. John seemed nice enough, but how unfair was it that he got to work here just because his father did? He would get to see Wanda every day that she was here, while I'd have to beg Nia to let me come back and visit and hope my parents didn't find out I was taking valuable time away from my stupid summer reading list.

Just then my phone buzzed. It was Nia; she'd just remembered that she'd promised to be at the studio all afternoon today to sign for a package, which meant it was time to go.

"Bye, Wanda," I whispered, pressing my hand against the glass. "I'll be back to see you as soon as I can."

8

The next day was Friday, and I knew if I wanted to see Wanda again anytime soon, it would have to be today. My mom didn't work on the weekend, and my dad tried not to, either, unless there was a plumbing emergency. That meant I would be stuck at home with them for two whole days until Nia took over again on Monday.

Nia understood, though she wasn't happy about going all the way out to the aquarium again. "We're spending more time on the F train than anyone should," she said. "I really want to finish my dolphin sculpture. And you've barely made any progress on your reading."

Oops. I hadn't realized she was paying that much attention. "I swear I'll read as much as I can on the train on the way there and back, and this afternoon, too," I said. "And I'll help with your sculpture later if you want."

"Fine." She sighed loudly, then gave me a sunny smile. "I can't resist you when you get all intense and passionate like that, Lilykins. But we can't stay long today, okay?"

"Sure." My mind was already jumping ahead to Wanda, wondering how she was doing, how her first night in her temporary home had gone. "Thanks, Nia."

When we arrived at the aquarium, Nia texted Dr. Hernandez, who sent someone out to let us into the lab. Nia looked around the huge main room with interest.

"Wow, it's pretty cool back here," she said. "Maybe you'll work here someday, Lily."

"Maybe," I said. *Unless my family has anything to say about it*, I added silently.

Dr. Hernandez was on the phone in one of the offices that opened onto the main room, and I spotted Dr. Gallagher talking to a man sitting at a microscope. And Ms. Butler—also known as Susan the grumpy water tech—was perched on a counter at a stool in the corner working with beakers and vials of water. Luckily her back was turned so she didn't see me.

In any case, I wasn't there to see any of them. My gaze went straight to Wanda.

The dolphin hovered near the bottom of the tank, her flippers moving listlessly as she just hung there in the water. I hurried over and whistled to her, though I wasn't sure if she could hear me through the thick glass. If she could, she gave no sign of it.

Nia glanced at the scaffolding I'd noticed the day before. "Maybe you should climb up there," she suggested. "Wanda might be able to see and hear you better that way."

"Probably," I said. "But I don't think I'm supposed to do that. I don't want to get kicked out."

Nia shook her head. "What's the harm?" she said. Then she added, "But okay, I guess I shouldn't encourage you to rebel so much. Stay here . . ."

She hurried off, returning a moment later with Dr. Gallagher. Nia was explaining why she thought I needed to get closer to Wanda.

"I don't know." Dr. Gallagher looked dubious as she glanced at me, then up at the metal platform at the top of the scaffolding. "Normally only the animal caretakers and researchers are allowed up there."

"It's okay," I said quickly, not wanting her to kick me out of the lab for causing trouble. "I understand."

"But Lily can communicate with this dolphin," Nia told the scientist. "Wanda responds to her— I've seen it!"

"Really?" The marine biologist looked me up and down. "Dolphins are known to bond easily with humans—it would be interesting to observe that with a wild dolphin in this situation." She glanced at Nia. "Are you her guardian?"

"Sure," Nia said. "I mean, I can give her permission to climb up there if that's what you mean."

I wasn't entirely sure my father would agree with that, but Dr. Gallagher didn't argue. "Okay, go ahead," she told me. "But be careful, all right?"

"Thanks." When the scientist hurried off, I smiled at Nia. "Thanks to you, too."

"Sometimes all you have to do is ask," she told me with a wink. "Now get up there and have fun." Just then her cell phone buzzed. She glanced at it. "Oops, I'd better take this. Come find me when you're ready to go."

As she wandered off, I climbed carefully up to the deck overlooking the tank. Wanda noticed me right away and drifted up to the surface.

"Hey, girl," I called when she stuck her head out. "How are you doing?"

The dolphin didn't chirp or whistle. She just floated there for a moment, staring at me, and then dived back underwater.

I frowned. She definitely didn't seem like herself. What could be wrong?

Before I could figure it out, I heard clanging from the metal scaffolding. It was John Hernandez climbing up to the deck.

"Hi, Lily," he said. "I heard you were here."

I nodded, glancing out at Wanda again. "She seems listless," I said. "Do you think she's sick?"

"She is, actually." John looked at the dolphin, too. "My dad and the others checked her over yesterday after you left. She has a mild bacterial infection."

"Oh, no!" I exclaimed. "Is it serious?"

"Not really. They already started treating it."

"Oh. Good." I slumped with relief. "So she should get better soon?"

"Yeah. I'll track her progress on my blog—I just haven't had a chance to update it yet. I'll make sure to put all the details up tonight, though." He shot me a slightly shy look. "I mean, if you want to read about it there."

"I definitely will." I smiled at him. "So do the scientists think that's why Wanda ended up in the Gowanus? Because she's sick?"

"Maybe." John shrugged. "I'm not sure. Dr. Gallagher thinks she might have gotten sick *from* the Gowanus."

I shuddered, thinking of the dirty water of the canal. "I wouldn't be surprised."

"Me neither." He laughed. "Anyway, they're hoping she'll be well enough for them to release her into the bay by Monday or so. Someone saw other dolphins out there again this morning."

"Her pod?" I said.

"Probably. I mean, it's not that common to see dolphins in the upper part of the bay. Maybe they're looking for her."

I shivered at the thought. "I hope they wait for her," I said, gazing down at Wanda, who was still floating quietly below us. Without even realizing I was doing it, I let out a couple of whistles.

John's eyes widened. "Cool. That sounded just like the sounds dolphins make!"

I could feel my cheeks going red. "Oh, um, yeah. I looked up some sounds and taught myself how to imitate them. I've been using them to try to communicate with Wanda."

He nodded thoughtfully. "People have studied that kind of thing before," he said. "Scientists once thought they might be able to learn dolphins' language. But it turns out that every individual dolphin has its own distinct whistle."

"Yeah, I've read about that." I shrugged. "Still, Wanda seems to respond to me."

He smiled. "She's probably impressed that you're making an effort," he said. "Hey, I never asked—how'd you spot her in the first place?"

I smiled back. John was really easy to talk to. He didn't joke around too much or act goofy like a lot of kids our age. In some ways, he talked more like an adult—a smart one who was interested in marine biology, like his father.

"It was Monday," I began. "I was waiting for Nia outside the hardware store when I looked into the water . . ."

I quickly relayed the whole tale. John listened quietly, nodding and smiling at all the right parts. "Awesome," he said when I finished. "Are you sure you don't—"

"Lily!" Nia's voice interrupted. "Hey, you done up there? I need to get back to the studio."

"Oh." I peered down at her. She was holding her phone, looking impatient. "Um, okay. I'll be right down." Then I turned to John. "Sorry, guess I've got to go."

We both climbed down. John said good-bye to Nia and me, then wandered off. Meanwhile I stepped closer to the glass of the tank.

"Bye, Wanda," I said softly, knowing she couldn't hear me but hoping she understood. "Work on getting better, okay? I'll come see you again soon."

A twinge of sadness shot through me as I realized I wasn't sure I could keep that promise. John had said that Wanda might be released on Monday. What if I couldn't get here in time to say good-bye?

I pressed both hands against the glass, staring at the dolphin, drinking in the sight of her—just in case. When I heard Nia clear her throat behind me, I took a deep breath and turned around.

"Okay," I said. "I'm ready to go."

Back at the studio, I tried to read, but I was too restless to focus. I got up and got myself a glass of water. Then a few minutes later I went to the bathroom. A few minutes after that, I was on my way to the kitchenette again to look for a snack when Nia looked up from her work.

"Hey, Distracto Girl," she said. "I thought you were going to read, read, read all afternoon. That was the deal, remember?"

"Sorry. I just keep worrying about Wanda." I'd filled her in on the dolphin's illness on the train ride home.

"Okay, I get it." Nia shrugged. "But at least you can keep one part of your promise. You said you'd help me with my sculpture, remember? Come over here and tell me if I'm getting the shape of the tail right—it looks weird."

I walked over to get a closer look. She'd made a lot of progress on the dolphin sculpture since bringing it back here on Wednesday afternoon. It was huge—almost as big as the real thing. Nia had used mostly stuff that most people would consider trash. In addition to the items she'd found by the canal, she'd added some colorful bits of wire and glass bottles, along with various other things she'd dug out of her Creativity Crate. But the way she'd put it all together into the graceful shape of a leaping dolphin made the trash look beautiful.

"It's pretty close," I said, studying the sculpture. "The flukes should be a little bigger, maybe."

"Flukes?" She shot me a quizzical look. "Can you translate that into English, please?"

I smiled. "That's just what a dolphin's tail fins are called." I pointed to the tail of the sculpture, which Nia had created out of two plastic food containers. "Right here, see? Each part is called a fluke."

She nodded. "Got it. Thanks. What about the fins or flippers or whatever they're called? Are they in the right place?"

"Close enough." I climbed up onto the first step of the collapsible step stool she used while working on larger sculptures like this one. "You didn't make a blowhole, though. That's how a dolphin breathes— it's pretty important."

"Good point." When I stepped down, she climbed onto the step stool herself, poking at the chunk of metal that formed the top part of the sculpture. "I can probably use wire for that. Oh! Or maybe the top part of a soda can—that would look cool, right?"

"Sure, I guess." I smiled at her. "I mean, I can tell you all about dolphin anatomy if you need me to. But you're the artist, not me. I can hardly draw a stick figure."

She chuckled. "True, I've seen you try to draw," she joked. "But that's okay—everyone has her own thing, right? Mine is art, yours is marine biology and stuff."

"Yeah." I sighed. "Too bad I was born into the wrong family."

"Huh?" Nia had already turned back to tinker with the sculpture, but now she returned her attention to me. "What did you say?"

"Nothing." I didn't want to complain. But I couldn't seem to help it. "I mean, it's not fair, that's all. John Hernandez gets to intern at the aquarium when he's only twelve because his father works there. Meanwhile my family thinks I'm crazy for wanting to be a marine biologist."

"Hmm." Nia sat down on the step stool. "I see

your point. Your family isn't exactly into the whole science thing."

"No kidding," I said with feeling. "My dad won't even let me get a goldfish as a pet. He thinks it'll distract me from school." I rolled my eyes, flashing back to all his lectures. "Meanwhile he barely finished high school himself!"

"That's probably why he wants to make sure you do better," Nia pointed out.

"Doubtful." I flopped onto the hodgepodge sofa, sending *The Call of the Wild* thudding to the cement floor. "It's not like Ricky or Ozzy are such great students, and he doesn't seem to mind that. It's just me."

Nia looked sympathetic. "You need to speak up more about this stuff. Make your family believe in your passion!"

"What's the point?" I grumbled, picking at a loose thread on a patch of bright orange silk on the sofa. "They'll never get it."

"Then you'll just have to ignore them and do what you want anyway." Nia hopped down from the step stool and went over to the Creativity Crate, digging around in there. "That's what I had to do."

That got my attention. "You? What do you mean?"

Nia straightened up, eyeing the dented soda can she'd retrieved from the crate. "I mean I haven't spoken to my mother since I moved out the day I graduated from high school. She didn't get it, either."

I didn't know what to say. Nia had never really talked about her past that much before. I mean, I'd known she hadn't gone to college or anything— just started doing art right after high school. But I'd been pretty young when she and Ricky had graduated, so I didn't remember much about it.

"What happened?" I asked.

"You know my mother raised me and my brother on her own, right?"

I nodded. I'd never actually met Nia's mother, though I'd met her younger brother a few times.

"She's an accountant, very practical," Nia went on, her voice sounding more subdued than usual. "She thought I should go to college and major in business instead of applying to art school. So even though I got into Parsons, she refused to pay for it. She thought that would make me do what she wanted."

"So what happened?"

She smiled at me. "You know what happened, Lilykins. I slept on a friend's couch for a while and got a bunch of part-time jobs until I could afford to support myself with my art. Mostly, anyway."

I nodded. Nia had sold a few of her pieces at craft fairs and the rest over the Internet. But she still worked a couple of shifts bartending on the weekends, and of course there was the money she got for watching me in the summer . . .

"Wow," I said, thinking that over. "Sounds like I'm not the only one who doesn't fit into her own family."

She smiled. "Don't feel sorry for yourself, baby—I sure don't. But know that you might have to make your own decisions about your life. Unless you want to let someone else make them for you, that is."

No. I definitely didn't want that. But I wasn't Nia. I wasn't gutsy and outspoken and strong like she was. I couldn't even talk to my best friends about how much they'd hurt me by not considering my feelings about the whole camp thing. How was I supposed to turn my life into what I wanted it to be?

It all just seemed like too much to figure out. Bending down, I fished *The Call of the Wild* out from under the sofa.

"Guess I'd better get back to reading," I mumbled, not wanting to think about the other stuff anymore right then.

9

Wanda was already on my mind when I woke up Saturday morning. I sat up and stared at the dolphin poster over my bed, my heart sinking as I realized there was almost no chance I'd be able to see her for the next two days.

I hope the medicine is working and she's feeling better, I thought. *Too bad I have no way of finding out . . .*

Then I realized there was one thing I could do to check in on the dolphin. I grabbed my laptop and pulled up John's blog, hoping he might have posted the update he'd mentioned.

There *was* a new post about the dolphin at the top of the page. But my heart flipped over when I saw the picture that accompanied it.

It was me! At first I couldn't believe my eyes; how had that ended up there?

Then, as I studied the shot, which showed me standing with my back to the camera and my hands against the glass tank staring in at the dolphin, I realized what must have happened.

He took my picture yesterday when I wasn't looking, I thought with growing annoyance. *He knew I wouldn't say yes if he asked, but he did it anyway, the sneaky rat!*

I clenched my fists, staring at the photo, a little distracted by how sad Wanda looked. Then my gaze wandered to the article beneath the photo. I scanned it quickly. It was pretty much the story I'd told John yesterday about spotting Wanda in the canal and the rest of it, though he hadn't used my name, instead referring to me several times as "Brooklyn girl" or "local resident" or something like that.

By the time I finished reading, I was fuming. How could he do this to me? I'd told him I didn't want to be on his stupid blog! Why didn't anyone in my life seem to care about what I really wanted?

I grabbed my phone, ready to send John an angry text until I remembered that I didn't have his number. Then I noticed another text waiting for me. It was from Julia.

Hey Lils, did you know Olivia C posted a pic of you? Are you hanging out with her while we're gone? Just wondering!

Several winky and smirky emojis followed. I scowled at the text. Why did Julia even care who I was hanging out with while she was gone? I was just Lily Left-Behind, right?

Then I sighed, my anger fading. This summer wasn't going the way I'd pictured it at all . . .

I was still distracted as I sat at breakfast a little while later. The whole family was there. My father had made pancakes, as he often did on weekends, and everyone except me seemed to be in a good mood.

"What's everyone up to today?" my mom asked, pouring my father more coffee. "It's such a beautiful day! Should we do something together as a family?"

Ozzy shrugged. "Sure; Mel's visiting her grandma this weekend, so I've got nothing to do."

"Glad you're so enthusiastic about spending time with us, son," my father said with a short laugh.

Ricky chuckled, too. "Great idea, Ma," he said. "We haven't done a family outing in a while. So what do you have in mind? Should we catch a movie or something?"

"Not a movie," my mother protested. "We should do something outdoors, take advantage of the nice summer weather."

My father shrugged. "We could see if there's anything going on at the park."

I was only half listening, already chafing at spending a whole day with my family pretending to be having fun doing whatever—while I was sure to be worrying about Wanda the whole time. Wishing I could be with her . . .

"I know," I said as a sudden brainstorm hit me. "Let's go to the beach!"

Four pairs of eyes turned toward me. "The beach?" my mother echoed. "Hmm."

"We haven't been out to Coney Island yet this year," Ozzy added. "Probably be pretty crowded today, though. Do you think it's worth the hassle?"

I held my breath as they all argued about it for a moment or two. In the end, to my amazement, they all agreed that it was a good idea.

"Okay, it's settled," my father said, slapping his hand on the table. "The Giordanos are going to the beach!"

My brother was right. Coney Island was crowded. Everyone in New York City seemed to be there— lying on the warm sand, playing in the surf, wandering up and down the boardwalk, lining up to ride the Cyclone. But my family found a free spot on the beach to set up our towels and chairs.

"Ah," my mother said, lying back in her folding chair and closing her eyes behind her sunglasses. "This is the life!"

"Come on, bro." Ricky poked Ozzy on the shoulder. "Race you to the water!"

The two of them took off toward the tumbling surf. My father settled himself beside my mother.

"You should go with them, Lily," he said. "Cool off in the waves."

"Maybe later." I tugged at the collar of the T-shirt I was wearing over my bathing suit. "I think I'll go for a walk first."

My mother opened her eyes. "By yourself? Maybe I should go with you."

I gulped. My plan wouldn't work if they wouldn't let me out of their sight.

"Relax, Deanna," my father said with a chuckle. "The girl's twelve, not two. She'll be fine." He squinted up at me. "Got your phone on you?"

I patted my shorts pocket. "Right here."

"Good. Then scoot." He made a shooing motion.

I obeyed before my mother could protest, quickly losing myself in the crowd. As soon as I was pretty sure I was out of my parents' sight, I made a beeline toward the aquarium a little farther down the beach.

It was pretty crowded there, too. Hordes of little kids surrounded the exhibits and the food carts. I headed for the door leading back to the lab, but it was closed.

I hovered there for a moment, not sure what to do. Why hadn't I asked Nia to send me Dr. Hernandez's number? I thought about texting her for it, but before I could, I noticed a familiar face nearby. It was Ms. Butler, the water tech. She was over by the shark exhibit talking to a couple of older women.

It was tempting to melt back into the crowd and wait for a friendlier person to turn up. But Ms. Butler looked more pleasant than usual. So as soon as the old women moved off, I hurried over.

"Um, excuse me, Ms. Butler?" I said. "It's me, Lily Giordano."

"Oh." Suddenly the pleasant expression was gone, replaced by her usual frown. "You're John Hernandez's little friend, right?"

"I guess so." I felt a pang of anger at the thought of John, but did my best to hide it. "I was just wondering how Wanda—I mean, the dolphin—is doing. Do you think I could come back and see her?"

"No, I don't think so." Ms. Butler's face and voice were as cold as the ice in the penguin exhibit. "Employees only."

"But Dr. Hernandez . . ."

I let my voice trail off. She was already striding away without a backward glance.

Feeling rejected and oddly guilty, I glanced at the employee door. Shut tight. If Nia were here, she'd probably try the handle, at least find out if it was locked . . .

But I wasn't Nia. So instead, I turned and headed toward the gift shop.

When I arrived, Eddy was behind the counter waiting on a young couple with two little kids. He smiled when he spotted me.

"Lily Giordano!" he cried. "Be right with you."

After the family left clutching their bags of souvenirs, Eddy waved me forward. "Hi," I said. "Sorry to bother you, but—"

"Bother?" he exclaimed. "Seeing you is never a bother, Miz Lily!" He winked. "I haven't even taken offense that you're spending more time off in that lab than you are visiting your old friend Eddy."

"You heard about that?"

"Sure I did." He smiled. "I figure that poor lonely dolphin needs your company more than I do."

"She does. I was hoping to see her again today. But that mean Ms. Butler wouldn't let me back, and I'm not sure how to get in touch with Dr. Hernandez, and . . ."

I stopped at his raised finger. "Leave that to me," he said, stepping over to the phone near the register. "I'll give Dr. H a call right now."

Before I knew it, I was stepping through the employee door. Dr. Hernandez had let me in himself this time. As we walked down the hallway toward the lab, I asked how Wanda was doing.

"She's much the same," he replied, a little crease appearing in his forehead. "Still rather listless and quiet. She doesn't seem to be responding to the meds just yet."

Panic shivered through me. "She's getting worse?"

"Not worse, no," he said quickly. "Just not noticeably better so far. That's a little surprising, but we're still hopeful. The good news is that she seems quite healthy otherwise. We think she's around three years old, so we expect she'll bounce back quickly once the drugs knock out the infection."

By then we'd reached the lab. I could see Wanda swimming sluggishly around her tank across the way. Thanking Dr. Hernandez, I rushed over for a better look.

The scientist was right. She looked the same as she had yesterday. Why wasn't she getting better?

"Hi, Wanda," I whispered, watching her swim around in a big, slow circle. "I just came to check on you. You need to rest up, okay?"

She didn't respond, or even slow down when she passed me. I followed her with my eyes, around and around the tank, wishing I knew what to do to make her better. What if the medicine didn't work? What would happen to her then?

This was why I wanted to study marine biology

one day. I wanted to be able to do more to help than just stand here watching and wishing and worrying. If only I could help right now . . .

I wasn't sure how much time had passed when a cheerful voice startled me out of my reverie. "Hi, Lily!"

I spun around. John Hernandez was standing behind me, his hands in his pockets and a smile on his face.

"You!" I cried, the whole blog situation rushing back into my mind. "How could you?"

He looked startled. "How could I what?"

"Put me on your blog!" I clenched my fists at my sides. "I told you I didn't want to be on it!"

"Oh!" His cheeks went pink. "Sorry about that. I started to ask you if I could include what you told me about finding her, but then your friend called you, and, well . . ."

"And you decided to go ahead and do it anyway, even though you knew I'd say no?"

"I didn't know that!" he protested with a little frown. "I didn't use your name or anything."

I couldn't believe he was actually arguing with me about this. "You used my picture!" I cried. "That's way worse!"

"I said sorry, okay?" he retorted.

"Well, that's not good enough!"

I didn't realize how loud we'd gotten until I saw Ms. Butler storming toward us from one of the side rooms. "What's going on out here?" she exclaimed. "This is a workplace, not a kindergarten class!" She pointed at John. "You're supposed to be cataloging those lab results. And you!" She spun to aim her finger at me. "You're not supposed to be here at all. Out. Now!"

"But—" John said.

"I was only—" I sputtered.

"Are you really going to argue with me?" she interrupted, glaring at both of us. "Go!"

I looked around for Dr. Hernandez, but he

was nowhere in sight. So I did as she said and left, tossing one last worried look at Wanda as I went.

Soon I was back on the beach with my parents. My mom looked up from her magazine, peering at me over the tops of her sunglasses.

"Did you have a nice walk?" she asked.

"I guess." Just then my phone buzzed. Another text from Julia.

Guess what we're doing after our scrimmage today? Field trip to the county fair up here! See? You should have tried harder to convince your fam to let you come. This is almost like that other camp anyway, duh!

I almost turned the phone off without replying as usual. But I was still worked up from what had just happened, and couldn't resist, my thumbs flying over the tiny keyboard:

Maybe you should have tried harder to notice that I don't like soccer. And I also don't like my

**friends doing stuff behind my back. Then maybe
you would know why I'm really not there.**

As soon as I hit send, my stomach went all
funny. Uh-oh. Julia hated when anyone argued
with her.

Oh well, I thought, lying back on my towel and
closing my eyes so my parents wouldn't talk to me.
Too late now . . .

10

By Monday morning I was itching to find out how Wanda was doing. John hadn't updated his blog since the post about me. Did that mean everything was the same? Or was no news bad news in this case?

Luckily Nia didn't argue too much when I begged her to take me to the aquarium that morning. "Fine," she said as we strolled down the street toward her studio. "We can head down there right after lunch. But only if Dr. Hernandez agrees to be in charge of you while you're there. I have something I need to do this afternoon anyway."

"Really? What?" I asked.

She turned away to watch a pigeon pecking at an abandoned burrito. "Just have to deliver a sculpture to a customer," she said. "No biggie. But this way I won't have to drag you along on my errand."

"Which sculpture? The one you finished last week?" I asked.

"Mmm." Nia had pulled out her phone and was typing on it as she walked. "Tell you all about it later, okay, Lilykins? I have a lot to get done this morning if this plan is going to work."

"Okay, no problem," I replied quickly, not wanting her to change her mind. "I'll stay out of your way."

Luckily Dr. Hernandez agreed to the plan. I spent the morning reading while Nia worked on the dolphin sculpture, which was just about finished. After a quick lunch at the falafel truck down the street, we headed for the aquarium.

When we got there, the place was buzzing with activity as usual. My eyes went straight to the tank on the far side of the room, where Wanda looked pretty much the same as ever. But Nia grabbed my arm before I could head over there for a closer look.

"Let's find Dr. H," she said. "I want to check with him about something."

A passing woman heard her. "You mean Dr. Hernandez?" she said. "He's in there." She pointed to one of the offices.

Dr. Hernandez was inside with John looking at something on a computer screen. When Nia and I stepped into the doorway, John glanced at me and then quickly looked back down. I frowned, not exactly thrilled to see him, either.

So I pretended to be fascinated with the contents of a tank of crabs and snails just outside the room as Nia talked briefly with Dr. Hernandez. The tank was bubbling so loudly that I couldn't hear what they were saying. But after a moment Nia popped back out of the room.

"Dr. H leaves at five thirty, so I'll make sure I'm back here to pick you up by then," she said, giving me a quick hug. "Have fun!"

"Thanks." I hugged her back, thrilled at the thought of having the whole afternoon to spend with Wanda.

As Nia left, I headed toward Wanda's tank. A boy was standing in front of it looking in at her. He was taller than John, with tousled reddish-brown hair. When he glanced back at my approach, I could see that he was maybe two years older than me.

"Hi," I said, wondering why I hadn't seen him before. He had to work here, right? Otherwise he wouldn't be in the lab. "Um, I'm Lily."

"Yeah? Good for you." He looked me up and down. "What are you doing back here? The kiddie tours are out front."

"I'm not here for a tour." I frowned, a little annoyed by his superior tone—just like some of the older boys in my neighborhood, who all thought they were so great. "Dr. Hernandez brought me back here."

Just then Wanda swam past where we were standing. She was moving slowly and didn't even glance my way.

"Do you know how Wanda's doing?" I asked, my annoyance suddenly swallowed up by worry. "Do the scientists think the medicine's working yet?"

"You mean the dolphin?" The older kid shrugged and rolled his eyes. "Who cares whether some dumb fish is still sick? Anyway, why are you asking me? You should ask your buddy Dr. Hernandez the Great. He knows everything, right?"

I took a step back, startled by his tone, which had suddenly tipped over from rude into down-right mean. "I—but—" I stammered.

But he was already hurrying away. A second later he disappeared through one of the side doors.

Huh? I had no idea what had just happened. Why had that kid acted like he had some kind of problem with me? I'd never even seen him before!

Taking a deep breath, I did my best to forget about the rude boy, whoever he was. I wasn't here for him, or for John Hernandez, or for anything or anyone else except Wanda.

I looked in at her, but she didn't seem to notice me. How could I help her if I couldn't even get her attention?

Then I had an idea. Dr. Gallagher had given me permission to climb the scaffolding before. That meant nobody would mind if I climbed up there again, right?

Soon I was up at the top, leaning over the lip of the huge tank. When I whistled, Wanda moved toward me immediately. She surfaced a few feet away, bobbing there and gazing at me with her dark, sad eyes.

"Good girl!" I called. "You remember me, right? It's your friend Lily! How're you doing, girl?"

I added a few clicks and whistles. Wanda swam toward me, and I held my breath, wondering if she'd come close enough to touch.

But no. She was already sinking back below the surface. I stuck my fingers in the cool water, wiggling them to cause a ripple. That attracted the dolphin's attention, and once again she stuck her head out of the water, though she was a little farther away now.

"That's okay," I murmured, glad that she was responding to me, even if she still looked sick and listless. "I don't need to touch you. I just need to know you're not giving up, okay, Wanda? You have to let the medicine work; you have to fight to get better. I mean it, girl!" I took a deep breath. "You have to. Because a lot of things in my life aren't going so great right now, and I can't stand it if one more thing goes wrong . . ."

Before I knew it, I was spilling my guts to the dolphin. First I told her about my fight with my two best friends, and how they didn't even seem to care that I was mad, since neither of them had responded to that text I'd sent at the beach on Saturday. That was no surprise, though. They hadn't cared what I thought when they'd changed their minds about camp. Why should they start taking my feelings into account now?

Speaking of people who ignored my feelings, I turned next to my family, telling Wanda how much I wanted to be a marine biologist and how little they all seemed to care. It was as if my dreams meant nothing to them . . .

I was just explaining about that stupid fifth-grade essay when I heard someone clear his throat just below me. "Eep!" I blurted out, so startled that I almost fell into the water. Peering down through the metal grille of the scaffolding platform beneath my feet, I saw John looking up at me from below.

"Uh, hi," he said.

"Were you eavesdropping?" I demanded, feeling my face go red hot as I thought back over everything I'd just said.

"No," he said quickly. "I mean, maybe a little, but I didn't mean to. I mean . . ." He paused and took a deep breath. "Listen, can I come up there and talk to you?"

"No," I snapped.

"Fine." He glanced in at Wanda, then back up at me, his face shadowy and hard to read beneath the metal grille. "Then I'll say what I need to say here. I'm sorry for putting you on my blog. I really am. I already deleted most of that post."

"You did?" I thought about that for a second. "Um, I guess you can come up here. If you want."

He didn't wait to be invited twice. It took him only seconds to clamber up the scaffolding.

"Thanks," he said, squatting down near the edge of the tank. "I really am sorry for doing that to you, Lily. I didn't get it, but I do now."

"What do you mean?" I asked cautiously.

He shrugged. "I thought using that picture was okay since I didn't show your face or use your name. Because I wouldn't mind if it were me, you know? But I talked to my mom about it, and she reminded me that everyone's different. And obviously you did mind, so I was wrong to do it."

"Oh," I said. "Um, thanks, I guess."

His face broke into a sunny smile. Then he glanced in at Wanda, who had just surfaced again nearby. "Looks like she's watching you," John said. "That's good. My dad's pretty worried about her."

Anxiety pierced my heart again, razor sharp and ice cold. "He is?"

"Yeah." John's dark eyes went serious. "She's still on those meds, and they should have knocked out the infection by now. But she's still acting sick, and nobody knows why."

11

Just like that, I forgot about what John had done, and about how embarrassing it was that he'd just heard me pour my heart out to Wanda about all my problems. The only thing I could focus on was what he'd just said.

"But why isn't she getting better?" I said. "Are they going to try a different medicine?"

He shrugged. "They're not sure what else to try. Like I said, the one they gave her should have worked. I think they even drew blood this morning to check on the level of infection."

"They did? What did they find out?"

"I'm not sure." John bit his lip. "They were still testing it the last time I checked. But that was like an hour ago, so the results might be in by now."

"How do we find out?" I demanded.

He headed for the ladder. "Come on, let's check the computer right now."

"Be right back, Wanda," I called to the dolphin, even though she was underwater now.

Then I followed John down the scaffolding and across the lab to the room where I'd seen him with his father earlier. Nobody else was in there at the moment.

John sat down in front of the computer and logged on. He was scrolling down the page when Dr. Gallagher poked her head in.

"What's going on in here?" she asked with a smile. "Oh, hello, Lily. I heard you'd be visiting us today."

"Yes." I was too worried about Wanda to make small talk.

Luckily John spoke up to explain what we were doing. Dr. Gallagher nodded.

"I ran the blood myself," she said. "The infection is gone. There isn't an obvious physiological reason why Wanda's not feeling better."

"Then why is she still acting like that?" I stepped to the doorway, looking out at the dolphin floating dully in the tank.

Dr. Gallagher shrugged. "We're still trying to figure that out. It's possible she has some sort of internal injury that isn't showing up in the tests." Just then someone called her name, and she waved and hurried off.

"I want to go back and sit with Wanda," I told John.

John nodded and followed me out of the computer room. Soon we were both atop the scaffolding again. For a while we just sat there watching Wanda swim listlessly around the tank.

Finally John broke the silence. "Maybe you should try doing some of those whistles you did before," he said. "She seems to like that. Maybe it'll cheer her up."

"Do you think so?" I felt a little embarrassed to do my dolphin sounds in front of him, but I also wondered if John was right. Wanda had responded to the sounds earlier, even if she wasn't as lively about it as before. "Okay, here goes . . ."

I whistled and chirped, and the dolphin surfaced, seeming to listen. Then John asked me to teach him some of the sounds. We worked on that for a while, and after a few minutes he could do them almost as well as I did. We took turns "talking" to Wanda, and for a few minutes she seemed almost like her old self.

Then when she began to look tired, John and I started talking to each other instead. He asked me how I'd become so interested in dolphins and sea life, and I asked him what it was like to get to spend all day at the aquarium. He was actually pretty easy to talk to when he wasn't posting secret photos of me on the Internet.

John was telling me about a marine biology conference his dad had taken him to once when he suddenly broke off in midsentence. His smile faded as he looked down at the front of the tank.

I followed his gaze. The same older kid I'd encountered earlier was standing down there looking in at Wanda, though he hadn't noticed us watching him. I was glad about that—I wasn't eager to face his obnoxious attitude again.

"What's he doing back here?" John muttered.

"He who?" I glanced at him. "Who is that guy? I thought he was an intern here. Like you."

John didn't even seem to hear me. He got up and clattered down the ladder, then rushed toward the older boy. The two of them faced off, both looking angry, though I couldn't hear what they were saying from where I sat.

I was about to move closer when my phone buzzed. It was Nia.

Got hung up in Manhattan, she texted. **Not sure**

I'll make it back to you in time. Can you call your dad to pick you up?

My heart sank. My parents had no idea how much time I'd been spending at the aquarium lately. They hadn't even asked about Wanda since that first night at dinner. Now Nia wanted me to ask my father to pick me up here?

I called her. "How late are you going to be?" I asked. "Maybe I can just wait outside until you get here."

"No!" She sounded alarmed. "If your folks found out I left you standing on a street corner in Coney Island . . ."

"Okay, okay." She had a point. "I guess I can call Dad."

I hung up and hit his number. He picked up after several rings.

"Lily?" he said. "You okay?"

"Sure, I'm fine." I took a deep breath. "But I kind of need a ride . . ."

I explained the situation—sort of, anyway. I left out the part about Wanda. Instead I let him think that my visit to the aquarium was a special treat from Nia because I'd gotten so much reading done.

"Hmph," he said. "She just left you there alone?"

"I'm not alone." I clutched my phone, not in the mood for an argument. "Um, she knows one of the scientists here, and he's watching me while she runs her errands."

"Whatever," he said. "I can come for you, but it'll be a while—we're at a job in Astoria."

I gulped. Astoria was in Queens, and at this time of day, with rush-hour traffic, it would be ages before he could get all the way down here. "Well, the aquarium closes in like an hour," I told him. "The scientists might be able to stay a little later, but . . ."

I couldn't make out what he said next since he'd obviously moved the phone away from his face. But I was pretty sure Nia's name was in there somewhere.

"Dad?" I said. "It's okay. I can take the subway home—it's not a big deal."

"No," he barked. "It's not safe."

"Sure it is, it's just the F train," I said. "I take it all the time. I know exactly how to do it."

I could hear John climbing back up the scaffolding behind me. "Who's that?" he whispered.

I lowered my phone. "It's just my dad," I said. "I'll be off in a sec."

When I put the phone back to my ear, my dad was talking again—something about him calling Nia to chew her out. "Don't!" I blurted out. "Listen, Dad, it's not that big a deal. I'll call her myself—maybe she knows someone who can come pick me up."

"You mean one of her crazy artist friends?" He snorted. "You'd be better off risking the subway."

John was poking me on the arm. I waved him away, but he only leaned closer. "Is Nia running late or something?" he whispered loudly. "I have an idea."

"No, it's not a big deal, I just—hey!" I said as John plucked my phone out of my hand.

"Hello, is this Lily's dad?" he said into the phone. "I'm John Hernandez—my dad is the head biologist here at the aquarium. Lily can come home with us if her ride is running late."

"John, seriously, it's no big deal." I grabbed for my phone.

But he dodged me, nodding at whatever my father was saying. "We live in Bay Ridge," he said. "You could pick her up there whenever you want." More nodding. "Okay, I'll get him, hang on."

He lowered the phone. "He wants to talk to my dad," he told me.

"Wait—" I began.

But it was too late. He'd already taken off, and a few minutes later it was all settled. I would go home with Dr. Hernandez and John, and my dad would pick me up at their place as soon as he could.

I thanked John for thinking up the plan, and then texted Nia to let her know.

Cool, she texted back a moment later. **Let me know if their house is decorated all in fish like your room, lol!**

I just rolled my eyes at that, then put away my phone and went back to focusing on Wanda.

I spent most of the rest of the afternoon on the scaffolding watching over Wanda. John had sat with me for a while, but then he'd had to go help feed the penguins out front. He invited me to come along and I was tempted to accept, but I decided to stay with Wanda instead. John seemed surprised and maybe a little hurt when I said thanks but no thanks, so I told him it was because I'd promised Nia I would read a few chapters that day—I even dragged my book bag up to the platform to make it more convincing.

I was kind of glad when he left and I was alone with Wanda. Not that I minded his company—he was a lot nicer than I'd thought after that blog incident. But I wanted to make the most of my time with Wanda. Maybe if I watched her carefully enough, I could figure out what was wrong with her . . .

Before I knew it, John was calling me down. "Time to head home," he said.

"Okay." I stood up. "Bye, Wanda," I called softly. "Rest up and feel better, okay?"

The dolphin lifted her head out of the water as I clambered down the ladder, keeping my eyes on her the whole time. I waved at her and smiled when she swam past the glass right where I was standing.

"She definitely recognizes you," John commented. He glanced at his father, who had just walked over to join us. "Dolphins get to know people pretty easily, right, Dad?"

"Yes," Dr. Hernandez said. "They are known to bond with humans." He smiled at me. "Ready to go, Lily?"

"Sure." I followed them out of the aquarium and across the parking lot. Dr. Hernandez's car wasn't fancy, but it was interesting. The hatchback held a smelly rope fishnet with dried seaweed stuck to it, a couple of large seashells, a single snorkeling fin, and a bunch of buckets, bottles, and towels. In the back seat next to me, a stack of books and magazines threatened to topple over. Most of them were about marine biology and oceanography.

John turned and saw me peeking at the pile. "You can look at those if you want," he said with a smile. "Right, Dad?"

"Sure." Dr. Hernandez glanced at me in the rearview mirror as he waited to turn onto Surf Avenue. "Help yourself, Lily."

"Thanks." I paged through some of the books and magazines as we inched through traffic. Eventually we arrived at a large old brick building in a nice part of Bay Ridge. Their apartment was on the top floor. When we entered, a woman with dark hair and cat-eye glasses hurried to greet us.

"Mom, this is Lily," John said. "She's the girl I told you about."

"Welcome, Lily," the woman said with a smile that looked a lot like John's. "It's so nice to meet you."

"Nice to meet you, too, Mrs. Hernandez," I said, feeling a little shy. How much had John told his mother about me, anyway?

"It's Dr. Duran-Hernandez, actually," John corrected me. "Mom's a scientist, too. Only she works for a company in Manhattan."

"It's all right," Dr. Duran-Hernandez said, shaking her head at John. "Lily, you can just call me Paula if you like—I know my last name is a mouthful!"

Dr. Hernandez chuckled, loosening his tie. "Did you order dinner?" he asked his wife.

She nodded. "It should be arriving shortly." She smiled at me again. "Lily, you'll join us, of course?"

I realized I was famished and nodded. That falafel lunch with Nia seemed like ages ago. "Um, thanks," I said. "If it's not too much trouble."

"Cool." John grinned at me. "Come on, I'll give you a tour while we wait for the food to get here."

12

Dinner was amazing. And I don't mean the food, although that was good, too—Greek takeout and a green salad that John's mother had made before we got there. No, the great part was the conversation.

When we all first sat down around the modern glass-topped table in the Hernandez family's dining nook, I wasn't sure what to say. After all, I barely knew them. Their lives were obviously nothing like mine, here in their fancy three-bedroom apartment with its doorman and elevator and views over the bay.

But somehow, I forgot about all of that as soon as they started to talk. They discussed such interesting stuff! First Dr. Hernandez asked about his wife's day. It turned out that she was a biochemist who worked for a company that was trying to invent new sources of energy. It sounded really interesting, and she seemed impressed that I asked her so many questions.

After that, the conversation turned to the aquarium. John and his father had been keeping his mother up-to-date on the Wanda situation.

"How's she doing?" Dr. Duran-Hernandez asked, spearing a piece of feta cheese with her fork. "Any better?"

Her husband shook his head. "It's hard to say. She perks up now and then—"

"Especially when Lily is talking to her," John put in with a grin. "Did you know she speaks fluent Dolphinese?"

I blushed as his parents both turned to look at me. "He's exaggerating," I said quickly. "I just try to imitate dolphin sounds, and sometimes Wanda acts like she's listening. That's all."

"Yes, you mentioned that before, I remember now." Dr. Hernandez nodded thoughtfully. "If Wanda is with us for long enough, we could do a study. Maybe we can figure out the degree to which she's responding to you. Could be interesting."

"Do you think she'll be at the aquarium much longer?" I asked.

John shrugged. "We can't release her if she's sick, right?"

I took a sip of water and thought about that. What if Wanda didn't get better soon? What if Dr. Hernandez and the other scientists never figured out what was wrong with her? How long would they keep her at the aquarium before giving up on her?

"I just wish we knew what was bothering her," Dr. Hernandez said.

"Me, too." I stared at my plate, suddenly not in the mood to eat anymore. "Do you really think she could be injured like you said before?"

"Injured?" John's mother put in. "What sort of injury do you suspect, honey?"

"That's just the thing." Dr. Hernandez sighed, fiddling with his napkin. "None of us can see any evidence of physical injury. She swims and breathes and eats just fine. It's just her attitude that seems off." He shrugged, his dark eyes sad. "Sometimes wild animals can't recover from being in captivity."

John suddenly dropped his fork with a clatter. "Or maybe Owen Butler is up to his old tricks," he blurted out.

"Huh?" I had no idea what he was talking about. "Who's Owen Butler?"

John's mother looked perplexed, too. But Dr. Hernandez was staring at his son. "Owen?" he said. "I thought I saw him at the lab today. But why would you think he has anything to do with Wanda's situation?"

"Because he's a jerk, that's why." John frowned. "And Lily and I both saw him looking in at Wanda today. Right, Lily?"

Suddenly I caught on. "You mean that kid you were talking to earlier?" I said. "Yeah, I saw him by the tank a couple of times. But who is he?"

"Owen started a student internship at the same time as John did this summer," Dr. Hernandez explained. "His mother works at the aquarium and convinced us to take him on."

"Oh, yes." John's mother nodded. "I remember you mentioning him. Susan Butler's son, right?"

Susan Butler—aha! That was the mean water-tech lady!

"Wait." My heart started pounding as I continued to figure out what John was saying. "You think that kid might be doing something to Wanda? Something to—to hurt her? But why would he do that?"

"Because he's a jerk," John said again. "That's why he got kicked out of the internship."

John's father sighed. "It was an unfortunate situation," he said. "Owen had to leave the program after less than a week."

"He was caught teasing the animals or something, wasn't he?" John's mother said. She stood and hurried over to the refrigerator to get more ice water from the dispenser on the front. "I remember you two talking about it at the time."

"Yeah, he was showing off for some girl by throwing popcorn at the penguins," John said, still frowning. "I told him to stop, but he wouldn't."

"Another employee noticed the same kind of situation the next day," Dr. Hernandez told me. "That was when we decided it wasn't going to work out."

"Wow." I thought back to the obnoxious boy and shuddered. "That's terrible. But why would he try to hurt Wanda?"

John shrugged. "He blames me for getting kicked out. So does his mother. That's why she's always yelling at me."

His father sighed again. "John, I've told you—"

"I know, I know," John said. "Let it roll off my back. She's a valuable employee." He rolled his eyes at me. "I'm trying, Dad, okay?"

For the first time, I felt a little sorry for John. Now I understood why Ms. Butler was so mean to John—and to me, too, ever since she'd seen us together that first time by the walrus exhibit. It couldn't be easy having to work with her every day.

"Anyway," John went on, "I wonder if Owen saw my blog and figured out that I was interested in Wanda. Maybe he wants to make me look bad by making sure she doesn't get better!"

His parents traded a dubious look. "I don't know," his mother said. "Sounds a little far-fetched."

"But he could totally do it!" John insisted. "Maybe he sneaked in and messed with her meds. Or maybe his mom is adding something to the water that's making Wanda sick!"

My mind spun. Could John be right? Had he just solved the mystery of Wanda's nonrecovery?

"John, let's not jump to any conclusions," Dr. Hernandez said gravely. "We can't just accuse someone of . . ."

He let his words trail off as a buzzer sounded. "That's the doorman," John's mother said, standing. "It must be your father, Lily. I'll have him come up so you can finish eating."

"No, it's okay. I'm almost finished anyway."

But it was too late. John's mother was already over by the door talking to someone over the intercom. A few minutes later, she was ushering my dad in.

He looked out of place in his work boots and sweat-stained shirt. "Thanks for looking after Lily," he said gruffly, shuffling his feet and twisting his ball cap between his hands. "I appreciate it."

"It was a pleasure getting to know her," Dr. Duran-Hernandez told him with a smile. "Would you like to sit down for a bit, Mr. Giordano? We have plenty."

"Thanks, but we need to be getting home. Her mother will be expecting us," my dad said. "Ready to go, Lily?"

My father and I didn't say much to each other

until we were in his truck. As usual, it smelled like sweat and plumber's caulk.

Dad started the truck. "Nice people, seemed like," he said, raising his voice a little to be heard over the roar of the diesel engine. "Glad they were there to take over when that Nia flaked out."

"She didn't . . ." I took a breath, forcing myself to stop. "I mean, yeah, they are nice. It was really interesting talking to John's parents about their jobs."

"Hmph." He shot me a quick, appraising look before turning his eyes back to the road. "Science stuff, huh? Yeah, I can see how you'd like that."

I was so surprised I wasn't sure how to respond. Was my father actually acknowledging my interest in science for once? And without making fun of it?

"Uh-huh," I said cautiously. "John is doing a student internship at the aquarium. Maybe next year I could do something like that. I think it's free," I added hastily.

"We'll deal with next year, next year," my father replied.

Maybe that wouldn't sound like a very encouraging response coming from most people. But my dad wasn't most people. From him, it was much more than I ever would have expected, and my heart leaped a little. What if . . . ?

"Hey," his gruff voice interrupted. "Where are your books? Didn't leave them at their apartment, did you? It's not too late to go back."

My books? I gulped, suddenly realizing something.

"Actually, they're not at the Hernandezes' apartment," I said slowly. "I think I forgot them at the aquarium."

I didn't just think that—I knew it. In my mind's eye, I could clearly see my backpack lying atop the metal platform by Wanda's tank where I'd left it.

My father scowled. "Are you kidding me, Lily? Your mother and I ask you to do one thing this summer, and this is how you act? I swear, for a

smart girl you sure do some foolish things sometimes. Now you're going to have to get that Nia to
schlep you all the way back out to Coney Island . . ."

I sank down in my seat, staring out the window and trying not to smile at the thought of going
back out to the aquarium—which my dad clearly
thought of as some kind of punishment. I also tried
not to let him see that I wasn't listening as he
ranted about my forgetfulness the rest of the way
home.

13

Nia was in a good mood when she arrived at my house the next morning. Luckily my dad and brothers had already left for their first job, so Dad couldn't yell at her about yesterday.

"So how was your visit with the Hernandezes?" Nia said as we walked across the bridge over the canal, heading toward the studio. "Sorry again for stranding you out there. I just couldn't make it back in time."

"I had dinner with John and his parents. It was nice." I started to go into detail, but she began whistling an airy little tune and didn't seem to be listening, so I stopped. What was with her?

Then I remembered what she'd told me. The reason she'd gone to Manhattan yesterday was to deliver a sculpture. Maybe she'd sold it for a lot of money. That would explain her mood, and maybe also why she couldn't get back in time. Maybe she'd had to go straight to a bank to deposit the windfall.

"I need to go back to the aquarium today," I told her.

She shot me a look of mild dismay. "Again? I'm starting to think we should just move onto the F train. Cheaper than an apartment, right?"

I chuckled along with her. At least she didn't seem mad.

"Yeah. For one thing, I forgot my book bag there," I said. "Also, I really want to check on Wanda. John had an idea about why she might still be acting sick . . ."

I filled her in on the Owen Butler theory. Nia actually stopped whistling and listened.

"Whoa," she said when I finished. "If that's true, Dr. H better put a stop to it!"

I definitely agreed with that. "So can we go?"

"Why not?" She tossed me a cheery smile. "Just let me grab my stuff from the studio and we'll head right down there."

When we arrived, Nia texted Dr. Hernandez. This time, John came to let us in through the employee door.

"I found your books this morning when I was helping to feed Wanda," he told me. "They're in my dad's office for safekeeping."

"Thanks." I wasn't really thinking about the books. "Is Wanda any better?"

"Wanda ate, though Dr. Gallagher said it wasn't as much as she'd like."

"Is there a bathroom around here?" Nia asked. She grinned at John. "It's a long ride out here, and I had three cups of coffee this morning."

"Right down that hall." John pointed. Nia thanked him and hurried off, leaving the two of us alone just outside the main room of the lab.

"Did your dad do anything about, um . . ." I glanced around the quiet hallway, half fearing that Ms. Butler might pop out and overhear. "You know—your theory?"

"Yeah." John's shoulders slumped. "Owen doesn't have anything to do with it after all."

"What? How do you know?"

"Because he just got back from New England yesterday," John said. "He's been up there staying with his dad and stepmom ever since he got kicked out of this place, and he didn't even know about Wanda until yesterday." He shrugged. "My dad says Ms. Butler was pretty insulted when he asked her about it. She said Owen might not do everything right, and yeah, she was kind of mad when he got kicked out." He took a deep breath. "But she said they both love animals—that's why she works here, and why he wanted to. She also said that's why they're so upset about him losing the intern-ship. He really wanted to do it, I guess."

I leaned against the wall, taking in what this meant. "So we're back to square one," I said slowly. "We still don't know why Wanda isn't acting right."

"Yeah."

John didn't have a chance to say anything else, because Nia was back. "Hey," she said, poking him in the shoulder. "Who's in charge of this place, anyway? Like, the head honcho?"

"My dad, I guess," John said. "I mean, he doesn't run the whole aquarium, but he's the head biologist, so I guess he's in charge of the lab."

"Cool. He around?" Nia grinned and winked at me.

I had no idea why she wanted to see Dr. Hernandez, but *I* wanted to get inside and check on Wanda.

When we entered the main room, Dr. Hernandez was standing right near the door talk-ing to Ms. Khan, the lab tech I'd met that first day at the canal, and a young man I guessed might also be a tech. The two techs hurried off just as we stepped into the room.

Dr. Hernandez started to turn toward his office, but stopped when he saw us. "Oh, hello," he said. "Lily, did John tell you he found your book bag?"

"Yes, thanks," I said.

"And thanks for looking after Lily yesterday, Dr. H," Nia said, stepping forward. "Here, this is for you."

She stuck her hand into her bag and pulled something out, shoving it into Dr. Hernandez's hand. I gasped when I saw what it was—a large wad of cash!

Dr. Hernandez looked startled. "What's this?" he said. Then he smiled. "There's no charge for babysitting. Lily mostly took care of herself."

"It's not for that." Nia stuck her hands in the pockets of her skirt, looking pleased with herself. "It's for this place—the aquarium. I just sold my dolphin sculpture that was inspired by Wanda, and—"

"That's the piece you sold yesterday?" I blurted out.

She winked at me. "Surprise!"

Suddenly I realized I hadn't been in the studio since yesterday morning—today Nia had left me standing outside while she ran in to get her stuff. So of course, I'd had no idea that the huge dolphin sculpture was missing.

John and his father still looked confused. "We camped out by the canal for a couple of days when Wanda was there, remember?" I told them. "Nia's a sculptor—she makes beautiful things out of stuff nobody else wants."

"Trash, basically," Nia added cheerfully. "And there was plenty of that by the canal."

"But how did you sell the dolphin sculpture so fast?" I asked her. "I mean, I didn't even realize it was finished!"

"I stayed up late the other night putting on the final touches," she replied. "And the sale was a lucky break. Remember how all those people kept stopping by to take pictures of Wanda?"

I nodded. I remembered that all too well. That was how my friends had seen me with Olivia Choi. It was a miracle that my brothers or parents hadn't heard that I was spending so much time at the canal.

"Well, a few people took pictures of my sculpture, too," Nia went on. "One of them sent a couple of those photos to a friend of his, who happens to be a rich art collector from Manhattan." Nia smiled. "The collector liked what she saw and made me an offer I couldn't refuse."

"Wow!" I'd known that the dolphin sculpture was good, but then again, I loved all of Nia's art. I was glad that other people seemed to agree.

Nia turned to face Dr. Hernandez. "So anyway, I want to donate half the proceeds to the aquarium to help take care of Wanda."

"Oh, I see." Dr. Hernandez looked stunned. "That's a very generous offer, Nia. Thank you. I only wish I could have seen that sculpture."

"You can." Nia fished her phone out of her bag. Seconds later, she'd pulled up a photo of the dolphin sculpture.

Dr. Hernandez studied it. "Beautiful," he said. "I would never have guessed it was made out of trash."

"I call it *The Lonely Dolphin*," Nia said.

I shot her a surprised look. "I didn't realize you'd named it," I said. "But that's perfect!"

"A little sad, though," John put in.

"Yeah." My gaze wandered toward Wanda, who was floating in the middle of her tank without moving much.

I stepped closer, leaving the others talking about the sculpture and Nia's donation. Wanda saw me coming and drifted a little closer to the glass, though she still looked lethargic.

"You *do* look lonely, girl," I told her softly.

Then I gasped. That was it!

I rushed back to the others. "I think I know what's wrong with Wanda! What if she's not sick at all? What if she's just lonely?"

"Lonely?" John echoed. "Like the sculpture?"

"Yeah!" Now that I'd thought of my new theory, I was sure I was right. "You said yourself that she acts a little livelier when I'm there talking to her. And your dad said that wild animals sometimes get upset about being in captivity. Plus everyone knows that dolphins are social creatures."

Nia laughed. "Maybe not *everyone*," she said. "But everyone in this room probably does know that, yeah."

"So maybe that's it," I continued. "She got stuck in the canal somehow and couldn't find her way back out. Now she misses her pod and is so lonely she's acting listless and sad."

Dr. Hernandez was nodding thoughtfully. "It's a good theory, Lily," he said. "If there's nothing physically wrong with her, it has to be something else."

"She's emotionally sick," Nia put in.

"So what do we do about it?" John wondered.

His father shrugged. "Actually, I was already thinking we might as well release her and see what happens." He gave me a serious look. "It might work out, or it might not. But her condition isn't improving here, so this might be her best shot."

I shivered, not sure whether I liked the idea of my theory getting put to the test that way. "When?" I asked.

"Are you around tomorrow?" he asked, looking at me and then at Nia. "Because if we're going to give this a try, there's no good reason to delay it any longer."

14

I set my alarm to go off early the next morning. There was no way I wanted to be late for Wanda's release.

My brothers were nowhere in sight when I stepped into the kitchen, but both my parents were sitting at the table drinking coffee. My father stood when he saw me.

"Lily," he said. "I was about to check that you were awake."

"Thanks, I'm up." I went to the refrigerator and took out the orange juice. "Nia's picking me up in half an hour."

"No, she's not." My father traded a look with my mother. "We're picking her up."

"Huh? What do you mean?" I asked.

He smiled, and I noticed that the corners of his eyes were starting to crinkle just like my grandpa's used to do. "I mean your mother and I are going to drive you down to meet the aquarium people," he said. "Your mother called Nia last night to let her know we'll pick her up on the way."

I was so surprised I almost dropped the juice. "You're driving me? Why?"

Maybe that wasn't very polite. But I was really wondering if I'd misunderstood somehow. Yes, I'd told my parents that the scientists were releasing Wanda today down near the Brooklyn Army Terminal, which was close to where the dolphin pod had been spotted. I'd had no choice but to tell them. Dr. Hernandez had insisted that I get their permission if I wanted to come, which of course I did want more than just about anything I'd ever wanted before. When we'd talked last night, my father hadn't said much, though my mom had asked lots of questions about Wanda and the aquarium and Dr. Hernandez and even John. She'd been the one who'd called Dr. Hernandez to give permission, though my father hadn't stopped her, which I'd figured was about as good as I was going to get from him.

Now my mother hurried over and plucked the juice carton out of my hand, then grabbed a glass from the drying rack by the sink. "We know how important this is to you, sweetheart," she said, pouring out a glass of OJ and setting it at my place at the table. "Your father and I had a long talk about it last night, and he decided to take the morning off so we could both go with you. Isn't that right, dear?"

He nodded. "The boys are covering this morning's jobs on their own," he told me. "Now hurry up and eat—we might hit rush-hour traffic."

"O-okay." My head still spinning, I sat down and stared at my juice glass. "Um, but you really don't have to do this, you guys. Nia and I were going to take the subway."

"Too hard to get to the waterfront that way," my father said, shaking his head. "You'd have to transfer and then walk. Besides, we want to help out—I mean, this is your thing." He shrugged, not quite meeting my eye. "I guess I figured that out when I saw you with those scientist people the other night."

Now I really was too stunned to eat. I'd assumed that the visit to the Hernandezes' place hadn't made much of an impression on him. Could I have been wrong?

"Dr. Hernandez said such nice things about you on the phone." My mother reached over and patted my hand. "He says you've helped them so much with this dolphin situation. We're proud of you, Lily."

"Th-thanks," I stammered uncertainly. Proud of me? For something like that—something I actually cared about? When had that happened?

Okay, so maybe my parents hadn't understood me very well all these years—hadn't always paid close enough attention to what I cared about, what I wanted out of life. Now I was starting to wonder if maybe I hadn't paid close enough attention to them, either.

But I would have to think more about that later. Right now, it was time to concentrate on Wanda.

The big flatbed truck from the aquarium was just pulling in when we arrived near the dock.

John was standing with a few other people, watching as his father and the driver maneuvered the truck closer to the water. "Hi," I said, hurrying over to join him. "How's she doing?"

"Same as ever, I guess." John smiled at me. "I'm glad you could make it."

"I'm glad your dad let you come along this time," I said, though I was a little distracted by the thought that Wanda was up there, in that big metal box, waiting to be released back into the wild.

"Me, too." John pulled out his cell phone. "I'm hoping to take lots of photos for the blog."

I nodded. The crane truck had just rumbled into view. It pulled over next to the first truck.

My parents were hanging back on their own, but Nia came over to join me and John. "Are they going to use the sling again?" she asked.

"Yeah." John snapped a few pictures of the trucks. "That's the safest way to move Wanda. Come on, let's go closer."

The three of us walked over to the flatbed truck. Dr. Hernandez lifted a hand in greeting.

"We're almost ready to go," he told us. "The crane operator just needs to get everything in position."

My heart thumped with worry and anticipation, and my gaze wandered up to the aquarium employees who were perched on the edge of the crate keeping Wanda moist and calm. "Can I see her before they lift her out?" I asked. "I, um, kind of want to say good-bye."

Dr. Hernandez looked uneasy. "I don't know, Lily. I'm not really comfortable letting you climb up that high—it's a bit risky."

"What if my parents said it was okay?" I crossed my fingers behind my back, suddenly glad that they'd insisted on coming today. "They drove me here, so you could ask them yourself."

Dr. Hernandez looked surprised. "They're here? Well, then let's go talk to them."

A few minutes later, it was all settled. My father and Dr. Hernandez had shaken hands like old friends. And my mother was all smiles as she chatted with him about how much I'd always enjoyed science and sea life. Wow! When had she started to notice that? All I'd ever heard were a few jokes about the "wallpaper" in my room. Once again, I tucked that observation away to ponder later.

A couple of the animal-care techs from the aquarium helped me clamber up onto the edge of the big metal tank. Finally I could see Wanda hanging in her sling inside.

"Hey, girl," I said softly. Then I let out a dolphin chirp, not even caring that the techs were listening. "I hope you had a good trip. You'll be happy when you see where you are."

At least I hope you'll be happy, I added silently, once again crossing my fingers.

"Hey, looks like she's listening to you," said one of the techs, a young guy with freckles and bright red hair who always seemed to be smiling. "I bet she's glad you came to see her off."

For a second, I felt tears welling up. But I swallowed them back. "Thanks," I told the tech. "I wouldn't have missed it for the world."

He nodded and traded a glance with another tech, a woman with a dolphin-shaped eyebrow ring. "You can touch her if you want," she told me. "Go ahead—it's okay."

"Really?" I gulped. I wanted to touch a dolphin—*this* dolphin—even if it was only this once.

Then I bent over, hanging on to the edge of the crate with one hand so I wouldn't fall in. I hesitated for a second, remembering the times Wanda had moved away before I could reach her. Was it fair to touch her now, when she was trapped?

Just then the dolphin let out a soft chirp. And somehow, that made me feel it really was okay. She wouldn't mind—not now, when we'd become such good friends. When I'd helped figure out how to make her happy.

I leaned in even more. I was just barely able to stretch down far enough to run my fingers down Wanda's back.

Her skin was damp, and warmer than I'd expected. It felt smooth and sleek, sort of like a rubber wet suit.

"Hi, Wanda," I whispered, too overwhelmed to speak any louder. "Hi, girl."

She wiggled in the sling, her flukes flapping, and I pulled my hand back in alarm. Had I scared her?

"It's okay," the female tech said. "She feels you touching her, that's all. Keep talking so she knows it's you."

"Okay." I cleared my throat. "It's okay, Wanda. It's just your friend Lily saying good-bye. Thanks for letting me touch you, and thanks for being my friend and being such a good listener. I hope—I hope—" I wasn't quite sure what to say next. So instead, I switched to Wanda's language, letting out a few more chirps, clicks, and whistles.

Then I heard Dr. Hernandez calling up to us that the crane operator was ready. The male tech helped pull me upright, and then other people were reaching up for me, helping me down from the truck.

"How was it?" John asked when I rejoined him and Nia.

I couldn't answer. I just shook my head and smiled.

"Dr. Gallagher said they put a tracker on Wanda," Nia told me. "That way they can keep tabs on where she ends up."

"I hope she finds her pod," I said.

Nobody answered, because just then the crane lifted Wanda up and out of her crate. She sailed through the air, out, out, out over the water of the bay. Then something on the crane shifted and the dolphin slid gracefully out of the sling and into the waves, disappearing instantly beneath the surface.

"Oh wow!" Nia said. "That was cool."

John started talking excitedly, but I didn't hear what he was saying. I stepped closer to the edge of the dock, scanning the water. Then I gasped.

"There she is!" I cried, pointing.

Wanda had just surfaced, her head bobbing in the bay. Then someone else let out a shout. It was the red-haired tech, who was still perched up on the crate.

"Dolphins!" he exclaimed, pointing a little farther out from where I'd seen Wanda surface. "Out there!"

Suddenly everyone was crowding the edge of the dock. Even my parents came closer, squinting against the sunlight reflecting off the restless waters of the bay.

There were at least a dozen dolphins, though it was hard to keep track as they leaped and skimmed over the waves.

"It's Wanda's pod!" John cried, raising his phone to take more pictures. "It has to be!"

I held my breath as Wanda turned toward the other dolphins. She disappeared underwater, and for a second my heart sank.

But then she burst into view again, arcing up and out of the water as she leaped toward the pod. "Yes!" I cried. "I think it really is her pod!"

"Yeah." John was grinning from ear to ear. "And she sure doesn't look sick anymore, does she?"

"No way." Nia clapped me on the shoulder. "Lily was right!"

Seconds later Wanda was with the pod, and after that I couldn't tell which dolphin was my friend anymore, not from this distance. They were a joyful mass of wet gray skin leaping and playing, and all the people watching laughed and chattered happily, and a few even applauded.

But I didn't make a sound. I wanted to watch her for as long as I could. Already the dolphins were getting smaller as the pod moved farther out into the bay, closer to the channel leading down between Brooklyn and Staten Island and eventually spilling into the open sea.

"Good-bye, Wanda," I whispered as I watched.

Once they were gone I still felt elated—but also a little sad. I wandered a short distance off from the others, thinking about what had just happened and what it meant. Wanda had really started to feel like a friend, and I didn't have enough of those lately.

Just then I felt my phone vibrate in my pocket, then again, and again. I'd brought it to take pictures, though I realized I'd forgotten all about it. Oh well. I was pretty sure John would share his with me.

I pulled out my phone and glanced at it. It was a series of several texts, and I almost put the phone away again, not wanting to spoil this moment. But something made me open the messages.

Hi Lily, it's me Amber, and Jules is here too, the first text read. **We've been talking, and we want to say two things to you. First, we miss you. A lot. We haven't been apart this long since kindergarten!**

I nodded as I read, realizing it was true. This was the longest the three of us had been separated since I could remember. Then I read the next message.

Anyway the second thing is we want to say we're sorry we switched camps without talking to you even though we knew you don't like soccer that much. We thought you would just go along with the plan anyway.

I grimaced. Of course they'd thought that! Good old Lily never complained, right? I moved on to the third text:

We believed you when you said your parents said no to soccer camp. Then we got your text on Saturday and we figured it out. You are the one who said no, right?

"Yeah," I murmured, both embarrassed and relieved. Why hadn't I told them the truth sooner? They were my friends—I should be able to tell them anything.

Anyway, the next text read, we want to make it up to you. So if you will forgive us we promise we'll spend a whole week at the aquarium when we get back!

I smiled. They got bored if they had to spend more than half an hour at the aquarium. I wouldn't make them spend a whole week there . . . probably.

Text us back and tell us you're not mad! the last text read. Please? Because you are our bff and we are REALLY sorry!!!!!!!! xxxxooooooxxxxxooooo A&J 😊♥

I typed in a quick response:

I forgive you! Busy now—ttyl OK?

As I hit send, John hurried over. "Hey, guess what?" he said. "My dad is over there talking to your parents again—and I think I know what they're talking about."

His grin looked sort of mischievous. I glanced toward my dad's truck. He and my mom were standing next to it—and sure enough, so was Dr. Hernandez.

"What are they talking about?" I asked John.

"You," he replied, still grinning. "My dad's pretty impressed by how much you're into marine biology, and how you figured out what was really wrong with Wanda. So he wants you to intern at the aquarium two days a week for the rest of the summer!"

I gasped. "Really?" I exclaimed. Talk about a dream come true!

Still, for a second I didn't quite allow myself to believe it could actually happen. What would my parents say?

But when I looked over at them again, my mom was beaming at Dr. Hernandez. And a second later, my dad grinned and stuck out his hand, and the two men shook.

I was still trying to take in what that might mean when John poked me in the arm. "That's not all," he said. "If you think it might be okay—and you can say no if you want—but . . ."

I was so surprised by how nervous he sounded—not like himself at all—that I turned to stare at him. "Spit it out, okay?"

He smiled sheepishly. "I was just going to say, it would be cool if you wanted to write a guest column about Wanda for my blog." He shrugged. "Only if you want to, though; it's okay if you don't."

My eyes wandered back out toward the water, and I wondered where Wanda was right now. Wherever she was, I hoped she was happy—as happy as I was.

"Sure," I told John with a smile. "That sounds like fun."

JOHN DORY'S JOURNEYS TO AN
UNDERWATER WORLD

By special guest blogger Lily Giordano

Hello, readers! As you might know from John Dory's last post, I'm the girl who found Wanda and helped release her. It was an amazing day! I was sad to say good-bye to my friend, and I still miss having her around. I think about her every time I walk past the Gowanus Canal, and lots of other times, too.

But that's okay, because I was really happy to get to see her reunite with her pod. (John already told you all about that, so go read his post if you missed it!) It's been almost a week now, and I get to help monitor the tracker they put on her as part of my work as a student intern at the aquarium. It's so cool! We can see exactly where the pod goes. Right now they seem to be heading toward the south shore of Long Island, so any readers in that area should keep an eye out for them—and if you see them, tell Wanda her friend Lily says hi!

Can't get enough fun in the sun? Read on
for an excerpt from Catherine Hapka's
DOLPHIN DREAMS!

The girl in the dolphin shirt glanced back once while Kady Swanson dragged her away like a cougar dragging its prey, but I pretended I didn't see. Who was she? Related to Kady, maybe? It seemed a likely guess, since I could see the family resemblance between the two of them—same bright blue eyes, raw-sienna hair, sharp little chin, and pale freckly cheeks. The only thing the new girl was missing was the haughty expression, which Kady used like a weapon at school, striking at those of us she deemed less than worthy. I closed my eyes and smiled, imagining drawing a cartoon of that, with daggers flying out of Kady's icy blue eyes . . .

"Maria?" a familiar voice called.

I opened my eyes and spun around, nearly dropping the book on my toes. Josie was striding toward me. Not walking, not ambling, but moving with purpose and energy, like the athlete she was. Josie never did anything without purpose. Or without the big smile she was beaming at me right now.

"I've been looking everywhere for you, *chica*," she said, tossing her sleek brown ponytail over her shoulder. How did her hair always stay so smooth and perfect, when mine exploded into a rat's nest the second it dried? We had the same mother, the same father. It didn't seem fair.

"I was just browsing." I tucked the dolphin book back on the shelf before she could see it and start asking questions. The last thing I wanted was to become the topic of conversation at family dinner that night, pinned in my chair like the moths and weevils in Nico's old childhood insect collection. If things worked out the way I hoped, well, the family would find out about it soon enough. If not, I figured they never needed to know.

I followed Josie out of the bookstore, glad to see that Kady Swanson and her cronies had disappeared. I was still a little bit curious about the dolphin girl, but not curious enough to risk the wrath of Kady. Even though the dolphin girl had seemed nice, she was with someone not-so-nice, which made me think she might be not-so-nice herself. As my *abuelita* liked to say, *"Dios los cría y ellos se juntan"*—birds of a feather flock together.

"Hey." Josie poked me out of my thoughts. "Are you daydreaming again, little sister? Wake up—there's a sale at the department store. Maybe we can find you a new swimsuit."

"I already have a swimsuit." I was tired of shopping. The air conditioning was too cold, making goose pimples dance up and down my arms and legs. The only reason I'd come at all was for a peek at those dolphin books.

"That ratty old blue thing?" Josie snorted. "Don't worry, Mom gave me money to get you a new one."

I wasn't sure why it mattered. Hardly anybody saw me in that suit. I avoided the busy public beaches, preferring my own company to the chaos of crowds. As my sister charged off toward the department store, I trailed along after her, dreaming about going to my favorite hidden cove.

* * *

Hours later, I finally picked my way down the steep, rocky trail leading into Spotted Dolphin Cove. That wasn't its real name—the place was so obscure it wasn't labeled on any map I'd ever seen. But I'd named it when I'd first discovered it two summers earlier. Since my friends Iggy and Carmen had moved back to Mexico with their family last year, I'd only ever run into someone else at the cove a few times. Most people didn't know it was there. The entrance wasn't easy to find and the trail looked like it led to nowhere. And even the ones who found it usually didn't like it—the beach was rocky and narrow, and there was no cell phone reception, and the water was too calm for anything but beginner surfing. But I didn't mind. I liked it for other reasons.

I dropped my surfboard and the backpack with my sketchpad and other stuff in it onto the rocky sand and stepped to the water's edge, letting the surf roll in and cool my toes. Squinting against the bright bursts of sunlight reflecting off the constantly moving water, I scanned the cove for signs of life. A gull was circling lazily overhead, letting out the occasional raw squawk. But that wasn't what I was looking for.

A smile spread over my face as I finally spotted a dorsal fin breaking the water. A second later the dolphin leaped up, arcing toward me, followed by another and another. I grabbed my board and waded in, not bothering with the leash. My parents didn't know I swam in the cove by myself, but then again, they'd never really asked. When I reached the drop-off where the water got deep, I belly flopped onto the board, paddling out to the middle of the cove with my arms.

The dolphins were close now—only the length of three or four surfboards away. I sat up on my board, dangling one leg off either side while I watched them play. How many were there today?

It was hard to keep track of the sleek gray bodies as they popped into view one after another. I recognized the one with the crooked snout, and the smaller, leaner one that I called Little Sister. The rest were just a blur of dove-gray grace.

Then I saw another familiar shape burst into view. "Seurat!" I blurted out.

This was the dolphin I'd seen the very first time I'd come here—the funny-looking one with white dots mottling his smooth dark skin. That first day I hadn't known why he looked so different from the others, but he'd reminded me of something a pointillist painter might have created. That was why I'd named him Seurat, after Georges-Pierre Seurat. The human Seurat was a famous French painter who pretty much invented pointillism, which is just creating images out of lots and lots of dots. If he'd ever painted a dolphin, it would have looked like my Seurat.

Later, I'd looked up dolphins online, trying to figure out if there was something wrong with my pointillist dolphin. But it turned out he was a whole different species from the regular bottlenoses he hung out with. As best I could figure, he was a pantropical spotted dolphin, a species that loved warm tropical water and so usually didn't come this far up the California coast, just north enough to make the water a little chilly once you left the sun-warmed surf line. But it seemed Seurat liked it here, because I'd seen him lots of times since.

I laughed as Seurat threw himself all the way out of the water, splashing down in a spray of foam and droplets that mixed with the white spots dotted all over him. He was always playful, even by dolphin standards.

"Show-off!" I called, wiggling my toes to stop my board from drifting sideways with the current.

I waited for Seurat to leap again, but after that one big effort he seemed content to float around and watch the others.

I did that, too, paddling with my hands and feet now and then to keep myself from drifting too far out from the beach. Not because I was afraid—I'd been swimming in the ocean since we'd moved here when I was four years old, and I felt as comfortable on my surfboard (or even just swimming) as I did on dry land. More comfortable, actually. Out here, I didn't have to worry about saying something stupid that would make mean kids like Kady Swanson laugh at me. Out here, there was nobody judging me or thinking I was weird because I didn't talk much and always had my head bent over my sketchpad. Out here, I didn't always remember to miss Iggy and Carmen, who'd left me adrift like a ship with no sails or engine when they moved away.

So being out on the water wasn't the problem, deep or shallow, but I still made sure to keep myself back from the dolphins. The dolphins were my friends, and I was pretty sure they liked having me around, but they got nervous if I came *too* close. I could respect that. I didn't like people crowding in around me, either.

After a while I noticed the sun was sinking lower out over the sea and realized it would be dinnertime soon. It was my turn to set the table, so I'd better not be late unless I wanted to hear about it from my mother. Reluctantly, I started paddling back toward shore.

"Bye, dolphins," I called to my friends. Most of them didn't pay any attention to me, but Seurat swam along behind me halfway to the beach, his funny spotted face popping up to watch me stand and catch a small wave back to shore.

When I got there, my sketchpad was falling half out of the bag where I'd dropped it, and I imagined it sending up disappointed feelings at me. I grabbed it and stuffed it back into the depths of the bag, telling myself it didn't matter if I hadn't done any work on my sketch today. There was still plenty of time, and I didn't want to rush it. No, it had to be perfect, and that took as long as it took.

In any case, it had been worth missing an afternoon's work to spend time with my dolphin friends. I whistled once in farewell, then grabbed board and bag and started the climb up the narrow, steep, twisting path out of the cove and toward home.

Sometimes you find a friend where you least expect it . . .

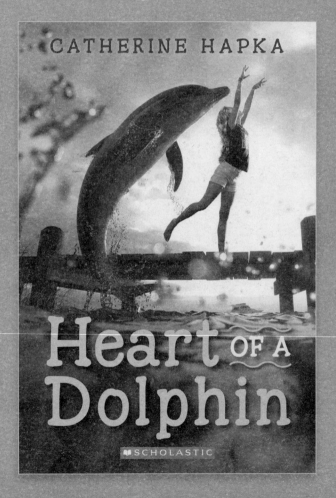

CATHERINE HAPKA

Heart OF A Dolphin

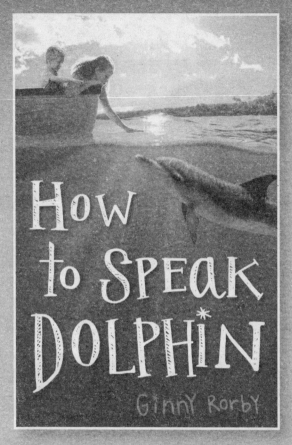

How to Speak Dolphin

Ginny Rorby

Nori, a captive dolphin, seems like the solution to all of Lily's family's problems. But Lily sees that Nori deserves to be free. Can she help the dolphin without betraying her own family?

Wendy Mass's birthday books are like a wish come true!

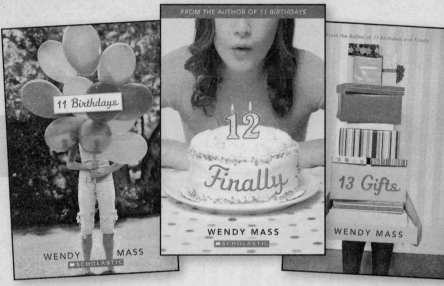

scholastic.com

**Available in print
and eBook editions**